CASTLE GOUT AND THE PECULIAR PETUNIA

Trussel and Gout: Paranormal Investigations No. 4

M.A.Knights

White Harp Publishing

To anyone who has ever lost their way home.

CONTENTS

38,000 words.

CASTLE GOUT AND THE PECULIAR PETUNIA

by

M.A. Knights

PART ONE

The Earl of York had a face like a man who was already dead: pale, yet blotchy; bloated, yet wasted. It was the face of a man who *knew* he was dead already, and was just waiting for the universe to catch up.

Mr Gout and I had been ushered into his bedchamber by servants who spoke in hushed tones. The entire household conducted their business in this manner, as if the sick man's illness had infected the very walls of the grand apartments in which he spent his final days. The only person seemingly unaffected by this gloom was the Earl's son, who followed us into his father's room and glowered under a storm cloud all of his own. He was not happy that we had been allowed an audience.

'My father is weak,' he said, his loud voice seeming like an angry cry. 'Make this quick.'

My master acknowledged him with a nod, then stepped towards the four-poster bed and its diseased-looking occupant. I followed, looking around the room with poorly veiled interest. It was, perhaps, unseemly to be goggling at a dying man's inner sanctum. But then again, just how often might I find myself in the bedchambers of the great and the good?

It was a stuffy room, decorated in the heavy style of the last century, when the queen was still on the throne. Paintings and prints in gilt frames adorned the walls, including a rather fine map of England. The bed was carved in a deep, almost black, mahogany, hung with thick, red drapes, long since faded in the scant sunlight that filtered into the room via its single window. I wondered at that. All that power, all that money, and yet the Earl was ending his days in a space little larger than the shop floor of my parents' small bakery.

'Who's there?'

It was the Earl himself who spoke. His voice was thin and reedy, though it still contained a note of authority.

'You have visitors, father!' his son called from his position by the door. 'You remember? Mr Gout and his…associate. You insisted they be admitted, against my–'

He was cut off by the Earl, who erupted into a bout of vicious coughing that shook the loose skin around his jowls, making him look, for a moment, like an ancient basset hound.

'Gout,' he said once he had sufficiently recovered himself. 'I knew a Gout, many years ago.

But this cannot be the same man?' He said it as a question, directed at my master, who had reached the bed and leant over it, so that its occupant might see him better.

The Earl peered up at the man through squinted eyes. 'But by god if you don't look just like him!'

'Hello, Jasper,' Mr Gout said.

There came an outraged sound from over by the door. 'How dare you be so familiar with his Lordship!'

'Oh, do shut up, Clarence,' the Earl muttered in his thin voice. He was peering at Mr Gout as though gazing upon a miracle. 'It is you,' he said. 'Though I fear to believe it. You look very well preserved for a man of our age. Remarkably well preserved. What's your secret?'

'Early nights with a good book,' Mr Gout said with a smile.

The Earl laughed at that, a noise like a cat bringing up a hairball. 'You always did have a wit.'

'I thank you for agreeing to see us,' Mr Gout said.

'I wouldn't flatter yourself too much,' the Earl replied. 'My world has shrunk, Gout. I've seen nothing but these four walls for near a year now. By god, it's a hollow thing, living to get old. Better to go out while you're hale and hearty, doing great things. Remarkable things. Then again, you seem to be weathering the ravages of Father Time far better than I. And as I recall, you did some

4

remarkable things, didn't you, Theophilius?' he asked, a queer look in his eyes.

'You were told why we have come?' was Mr Gout's only response.

The Earl nodded slowly. 'You have a question for me, I believe? But first, you must introduce me to your charming young companion!'

'Ah, forgive my rudeness,' said my master, and placed a hand on the small of my back, gently propelling me closer to the side of the Earl's sickbed. 'This is Miss Clementine Trussel, my apprentice.'

The Earl peered up at me with interest. I sketched a hasty curtsey, unsure of the correct protocol for meeting an Earl, especially one in his nightdress.

'Apprentice, is it?' he said. 'Remind me, Theophilius, which trade are you involved in?'

'I suspect if you remember my face, you remember that too, Jasper.'

The Earl sucked a tooth, thoughtfully. 'Aye,' he said. 'I believe I do. Which I suppose brings us back to your question.'

'It does.'

'Well, out with it, man. I am subject to time, even if you, apparently, are not.'

Mr Gout was silent for a moment. 'It is really a very simple question,' he said eventually.

'I'm all ears.'

'Where do I live, Jasper?'

The Earl looked at him. 'What?'

'My house. The ancestral seat of my family. Do you remember where it is?'

The Earl's brow furrowed. 'Is this some sort of joke? Not that I mind particularly. God knows, my opportunities for amusement are precious few these days.'

'No joke, my lord.'

'I see. Dare I ask why you cannot remember where your own house is?'

'I have met with some…complications. They have prevented me from remembering.'

'Complications? Tell me, would these complications be of a similar nature to those involving Matthias? Nasty business, that.'

I felt my master stiffen at the name.

Matthias, I had recently learnt, was the name of Mr Gout's brother. His dead brother. His dead brother who had returned as a revenant, an angry spirit, only to be defeated and sent on to whatever comes next by Mr Gout, when my master was still just sixteen or so. Little older than I was then.

Mr Gout appeared to consider his next words carefully. 'The matters are not connected, so far as I know,' he said. 'But they are, perhaps, similar in nature, if that is what you mean.'

'Supernatural, then.'

Mr Gout seemed a little taken aback by that. 'Indeed,' he said. 'Though, forgive me; as I recall, you were never particularly convinced of my thoughts in that regard.'

'I wasn't. Thought you a bloody fool, if you want the truth. A madman, maybe.'

'And now?'

'I have lived a long life, Gout. A very long life. Things that seemed clear to me in my youth now seem…less so. Besides,' and here he lifted his arm in a weak gesture towards his son, still lurking by the door. 'If Clarence here is to be believed, you've come fresh from vanquishing another angry, dead thing. A member of my own staff, no less!'

The Earl's son scowled, but said nothing.

Mr Gout nodded. 'It is true.'

'Fascinating. None of this, however, explains why you have apparently forgotten where you live.'

'As I said, I have suffered some–'

'Complications, yes,' said the Earl.

'Will you help me?'

'A better question might be, *can I help you*?' A thin smile twisted his face. 'I am not the man I once was, Theo. I have complications of my own. More mundane, I suspect, than your own, but no less powerful for that.'

Mr Gout frowned. He looked about to speak, but shut his mouth instead and remained silent.

The Earl laughed again. A wheezy chuckle. 'A funny life, isn't it, Theo? Here you are, after all these years, master of occult magics, yet still you come begging to me for help.'

I watched my master's face colour. It was unnerving to see him be rattled by simple words.

I couldn't help but wonder about the exact nature of the relationship these two men enjoyed, back when they were young men together at Oxford.

When Mr Gout spoke, his words were stiff. 'If you will not help, then–'

'Oh, calm yourself, Theo!' the Earl cut him off. 'I never said that. As it happens, I can help. Many facts I once held tight now escape me, but I fear I would have to live a further eighty-six years before I forgot the name of the notorious Castle Gout. Or the village in which it is located. I will say this for you, Gout; you leave an impression.'

Mr Gout said nothing, but I could feel him holding his breath.

'Well?' he eventually said with a gasp. 'Are you going to tell me or not?'

The Earl smiled. I got the impression he had been waiting for his old friend to crack. 'Morton-Upon-Mere,' he said. 'That is where you will find your erstwhile abode.'

I looked to my master, expecting to see some kind of reaction. Joy? Relief? I wasn't sure. But he continued to frown with tense expectation.

'Where?'

'Morton-Upon-Mere,' the Earl repeated.

But Mr Gout shook his head. 'I don't...I can't hear you.'

'Must I shout?' the Earl said tetchily.

'He said Morton-Upon-Mere, Mr Gout,' I said.

But he looked at me, still confused. 'I cannot...I can't make it out. The name...it's as if the words are obscured.' He sagged then, weary, all at once. 'The curse.'

I saw the Earl's eyebrows rise. 'A curse, is it? My, my, Gout. Don't you live an exciting life? I could point to it on a map, if that might help? You, girl, fetch that picture.'

This last was to me, and he waved an exhausted arm toward the map I had been admiring when we walked in. I chose to ignore being referred to as *girl*, supposing that, as an Earl, the man had become accustomed to referring to people however he so chose. Instead, I did as I was bid. The glass on the map was thick with dust. Did the Earl have no housemaids? I held back a sneeze and gently placed the thing on the bedclothes across the Earl's lap, careful not to be too rough in case I accidentally hurt him. The old man gazed at the map for a moment, his eyes searching, then he stabbed at it with a gnarled finger, white as bone.

'There,' he said.

I bent to look at where he was pointing. 'I don't see it.'

'Well, it's not written down, girl,' the Earl said as if I were a simpleton. 'It's just a village. Too small to be of any real significance. But that's where you'll find it.'

I examined the area around where he had pointed. His finger had come to rest just on the edge of Dartmoor, a place I had heard wild tales of, but never been to. 'It's in Devon, sir,' I said to Mr Gout, who was peering over my shoulder.

'Somewhere between a town called Blackmoor Gate and Parracombe.'

'Do you think you can remember that, Clementine, dear?' he said, closing his eyes and massaging them with his thumb and forefinger. 'I fear every time I look, it gives me the most frightful headache.'

'I...I think so,' I said, sounding very much like I thought nothing of the sort. Maps are like that. It all looks so very ordered and obvious while you look at one, but turn your head for a second and it all disappears.

'Take the map with you, if you like. Look, we can mark the spot with this,' said the Earl, handing me a letter opener that had been lying on the blankets.

'Father, that map is worth–' But Clarence's protestations were cut short once again by a vicious look from his father.

I hesitated, unsure what he expected me to do. The Earl tutted with annoyance.

'Well go on, girl, scratch the point on the glass.'

I looked to my master, who gave a small nod. 'This is very generous of you, Jasper,' he said, turning back to the Earl, who waved away the comment with a twitch of his fingers.

'It's nothing.'

'How can I repay you?' Mr Gout asked.

The Earl looked at him then, examining my master's face as if seeing it for the first time. 'You can go and live, Theo,' he said. 'I'll be dammed if I know what sorcery has you standing there, hale and hearty, while I wither away in this accursed bed, but whatever it is, go and make the best of it! Youth and health are generally wasted on those who have them. So go. Do remarkable things.'

My master bowed. 'I shall certainly endeavour to do my best.'

The Earl grunted. 'Now leave me,' he said. 'I need to rest.'

We were ushered from the room without ceremony. The lights in the hall outside seemed bright after the gloom of the dying man's boudoir, and we stood for a moment, blinking in the glare. I held the map awkwardly under one arm.

'Well, you've got what you came for,' the Earl's son said, frowning at us. 'Now please leave before my addled father decides to give you any more of our art collection.'

Mr Gout regarded him with distaste. 'With pleasure,' he said, and began to walk away, but stopped, as if something had just occurred to him. 'Do you know,' he said to the son of the Earl, 'When we first met I felt you reminded me of someone, and I've finally realised who it is.'

'Oh?' said the man, looking bored. 'Who?'

'Your father,' Mr Gout said, with a bright little smile. 'When he was a younger man, of course. Well, we won't take up any more of your precious time. We can see ourselves out. Toodles!'

As my master strode away, I saw the Earl's

son's face go white. To this day, I do not think Mr Gout could have left him with a more vicious parting blow, even if he said the man had reminded him of a troll.

PART TWO

Devon, it turned out, was fine country. Our wagon trundled down narrow lanes, sided by great banks of lush grass, dotted with spring flowers of yellow and pink. The fields beyond were vibrant with fresh growth. I had enjoyed the journey. Winter, it seemed, had gone on for far longer than it had any justifiable right to do, and I was glad of the March weather. The sun, though still weak, felt warm on my cheek and the sky was blue for the first time in many weeks. But not all of my travelling companions felt the same swell of joy at the coming of spring.

'It's freezing!' grumbled Mrs Winchester, clutching at her shawl and pulling it tighter around her bony shoulders. She glared out at the scenery as though it had insulted her cooking.

'You can have my blanket, if you like,' I offered.

She scowled at me, but took the blanket when I held it out. She draped it across her lap, then took my hand and patted it affectionately. I bit back a laugh.

The change in Mr Gout's old housekeeper's attitude towards me in the weeks since we had first met was immense, if subtle to the outside observer. When I had first arrived at Oystercatcher Cottage to take up my position as Mr Gout's apprentice, she had treated me with poorly concealed distaste. It had taken some work to win her trust, but it seemed I had been successful in doing so. She still often treated me with distaste, but no more so than she treated anyone else, and every now and again she let slip a little sign of grudging affection.

She hadn't been keen on leaving her home, but she had been adamant that we would not be making the trip to Morton-Upon-Mere without her.

'You'll need me,' she had insisted, loudly and often as we prepared for the journey. 'Just see if you don't. How long has it been? Fifteen years? Thirty? That's a house that'll need a woman's touch, believe you me. I know you, Theophilius Gout, one wave of a feather duster and you'll be overcome. No, it's no good. I shall simply have to come along with you.'

Mr Gout had put up a token resistance, but I suspected he was glad of her enthusiasm. Her coming, however, had unintended consequences.

'Well, I don't hold with it!' It was Klous the Kobold who muttered this from his position perched atop the luggage at the back of the wagon. It was about the tenth time he'd said something similar in the last hour.

'It ain't natural, if you ask me,' he added, when no one replied. 'Too much grass. Give me the sea any day of the week!' He sank his frog-like face into the collar of his tatty raincoat so that only his huge, round eyes could be seen. His wellington-clad feet swung disconsolately.

Klous had definitely not wanted to come.

The Kobold had once been a Klabautermann, a sea-faring member of his race, and was still getting used to being landlocked. It had been bad enough in Abermwyl, with the sea all around and the sound of the waves a constant companion to all who lived there. Travelling inland had been a challenge for the little creature. There'd been nothing for it, though, not really. With Mr Gout, Mrs Winchester and myself all leaving Oystercatcher Cottage, Klous was not about to be left behind.

'Quit your whinging and make yourself useful,' Mrs Winchester said, quite unsympathetic. She fished about in a wicker bag at her side and pulled out a sleeping rabbit that glowed with blue-green light. I could see her hands right through its translucent body. 'He's been nibbling at the sandwiches and I'll not have him do it again when next he wakes. You take him for a bit.'

She thrust the rabbit towards the Kobold,

who accepted him with a tut of annoyance.

'An' what am I sposed to do with 'im, ay?'

'Charm him with your winning personality,' the housekeeper suggested.

The rabbit was called Custard, and he was dead. Despite this, he was the only one of my companions who had done no complaining at all. Returned as a poltergeist, he seemed none the worse for his demise. In fact, Mr Gout assured me he was in better health now than he had been for years.

Mr Gout turned from his seat on the front of the wagon to face us. 'Did I hear someone mention sandwiches?' he said, his face hopeful.

'No, you didn't!' Mrs Winchester snapped. 'Don't think I didn't notice you filch one earlier, you great glutton. There'll be no sandwiches in your future, my good man. Not until we get to Morton-Upon-Mere at any rate.'

Mr Gout's face fell.

'You can have mine,' Klous offered, making a face and sticking out a large black tongue. 'I've tasted bilge water more appetising than whatever offence t' decency you put in them sandwiches we 'ad yesterday.'

Mr Gout beamed. 'Do you really mean it? Why, you really are the most splendid Kobold I ever met!'

'I'm the only Kobold you ever met.'

'And what a credit to your species you are!'

Mrs Winchester's face looked like she'd been

drinking bilge water herself. 'Why, you ungrateful little toad! I'll have you know that was potted ham, that was, *and* mustard!'

'Only thing potted around here is your head, you old crone,' Klous mumbled.

'*What was that?*'

'How far away are we now, do you think?' I said in a loud, bright voice.

But Mrs Winchester would not be distracted. 'You ought to be a sight more grateful,' she said, waggling a thin finger in the Kobold's direction.

Klous bridled. 'Oh yeah? Why's that?'

'Because when we get home, I've a good mind to banish you back to the woodshed!'

'Let's not fight,' I said, knowing it was hopeless.

Klous narrowed his bulbous eyes. 'You wouldn't dare!'

'Try me, you overgrown tadpole!'

I sighed and tuned them out as they continued to hurl insults at each other. Mr Gout caught my eye and winked, his blue eyes sparkling, then turned back to face the road.

They had been at it like this for most of the journey. In truth – and both would quite possibly have rather died than admit it, especially to the other – they had settled into a sort of grudging mutual respect back at Oystercatcher Cottage. But the open road seemed to bring out the worst in them. I sometimes suspected Mr Gout of deliberately fanning the flames.

My master had seemed in a strange mood since the day we visited the Earl. On the surface, he was his usual jovial self: quick with a smile, swifter with a laugh. Even more playful than normal, in fact. But I had been watching him carefully – something I did more and more – and when he thought no-one was looking, he slipped into a thoughtful, melancholy silence. It was the curse, I reasoned. He was anxious about the possibility it might finally be lifted after all these years. We might actually find some solid, tangible evidence of what had happened to him.

#

We rolled into Morton-Upon-Mere at around midday. The Earl had been right about at least one thing: it was hardly a metropolis. We appeared from one of three roads that led towards what was obviously the village green, a triangle of grass on which stood a bench, a large oak tree, and a single dun-coloured chicken. The chicken clucked off about business of its own as we approached, leaving us alone in the deserted heart of the village. Roads that ringed the green were themselves ringed by buildings of various types. The most notable of these was a church with a tower, which stood behind high stone walls. A little path, lined with ancient yew, led through a cluster of graves up to the large wooden doors. They were closed, in a firm, locked-looking kind of way.

Directly opposite the church was an inn. The swinging sign had a picture of a plant with long, spear-shaped green leaves and small white flowers. The delicately painted gold letters read 'The Wild Garlic'. Its doors were also closed.

There were various other buildings facing onto the green, but our attentions were naturally drawn to the only one with a door that stood open. It was a squat white building with a rose growing by the side of the door that was just beginning to show signs of fresh growth. A sign out front announced it as 'Mrs Popkins Tea Shop'. I glimpsed someone moving inside.

'You people bring me to all the liveliest places,' Klous muttered. 'Why couldn't I have come with you to see the Earl? I bet there was more going on there!'

Nobody answered him. I was too busy thinking about what we should do next. We needed to find Castle Gout. That meant asking questions. Asking questions might prove... complicated. Would anyone here remember Mr Gout? If they did, it might be hard to explain where he'd been all these years, not to mention why he appeared to be roughly half the age he ought to be.

'What should we do now?' Mrs Winchester asked. She was looking down her nose at the little village, her lips pursed.

'I'd say that was obvious, my dear,' said Mr Gout with a smile. 'We should get a cup of tea!'

Mrs Winchester rolled her eyes but she didn't disagree.

'Is that a good idea?' I asked. 'I mean, we don't really know what kind of reception we're likely to get.'

'Tea is always a good idea,' Mr Gout announced cheerfully. 'As for what kind of reception we shall receive, there is only one way to find out for sure, and that is to receive it.'

'Well, I know exactly what sort of reception *I'll* receive,' Klous said. Indeed, he had already hunkered down among our cases and was looking out fretfully for signs of life.

'True,' Mr Gout admitted. 'Perhaps you had better stay with the wagon. You can watch Custard. I suspect he may also cause the good people of Morton-Upon-Mere some consternation.'

'It's not fair!' Klous whined, pulling a pout.

'I'll buy you a scone,' I promised. 'If they have them.'

The little creature brightened considerably. 'With that stuff that goes on top?'

'Clotted cream?'

'Yeah! And jam, don't forget the jam!'

'Who could forget the jam on a scone?' Mr Gout asked, looking horrified at the very thought.

'Are we going in or what?' Mrs Winchester snapped, clearly growing impatient.

So we tethered our horse to the bench on the green, left Klous with the sleeping Custard, and ventured through the open doorway of Mrs

Popkins' Tea Shop. We entered a room with a low ceiling, crossed with stout timbers painted black. There was a well-swept wooden floor, a selection of furiously polished tables and chairs (the whole place smelt, not unpleasantly, of beeswax), and a small fire, burning in a large fireplace. It struck warm as we entered.

There was a portly woman behind the counter, serving a customer with her back to us. They both turned to look as we entered. The portly woman – Mrs Popkins herself, perhaps – smiled and said, 'Be right with you, dearies!', then turned back to the lady she had been conversing with. The second woman was of the solid, farmer's wife build I was used to from Fairsop. She had forearms I had no doubt were capable of manhandling a stubborn ewe in and out of a dip when called to, but her hairstyle was curled into a tight bun of respectability. Sh elooked to in around her sixtieth year, or perhaps a little older.

She was staring at us as if she had seen a ghost.

I almost looked around, fearing I'd see Custard crouched behind us, but then I realised it was Mr Gout she was looking at.

Oh dear.

Her mouth fell open and she flapped it a few times. The woman behind the counter looked at her with concern. 'You all right, Deirdre, love?'

Deirdre made a small gurgling sound. Then, tearing her head away from us, said 'Fine...fine.

Um...how much did you say?'

The other woman gave her a bemused smile. 'You've already paid, dear. Here's your scones and fruit loaf.' She pushed a brown paper package across the counter.

Deirdre stared at it. Stared through it. 'Right,' she muttered. 'Right. Fruit loaf.'

Then she shot another look in our direction. 'Well, thank you, Mrs Popkins, I'll...I'll see you later.' Then she hurried past us, shooting Mr Gout another frightened look as she passed, and disappeared out of the door.

'Wait!' Mrs Popkins cried. She held up the package, which had been left untouched on the countertop. But there was no response.

Mrs Popkins chuckled, placing the package of scones and fruit loaf back on the counter. 'Dear oh dear, what's got into her? Forget her own head next, poor woman.'

'Do you want me to run after her?' I offered.

The woman smiled at me. 'Well, aren't you kind, but no need to worry, love. I'll send our Simon round to the farm after lunch. Now!' She clapped fat hands together. 'What can I do for you three? I don't believe I've seen you around here before. Are you passing through? Or is it board you're looking for?'

'Actually, we're looking for–' I began, but Mr Gout cut me off.

'We're looking for some tea!' he announced, bouncing excitedly on his heels. 'And perhaps a

22

cake or two? Oh, and some scones, of course!'

Mrs Popkins grinned broadly. 'Well then, my dears, you've come to the right place! Tea and cake are my bread and butter, so to speak. You just seat yourselves wherever you feel most comfortable and let old Mrs Popkins look after you.'

We chose a table close to the fire, for although it had seemed warm when we first came in, we were already missing the sun's heat. Spring might well be on its way, but winter hadn't quite left us. Mrs Popkins bustled around us, arranging plates and cutlery, wiping imaginary dust from tea cups, straightening the tablecloth, and generally bestowing on us every bit of care and attention that she could. It must be a quiet day, I supposed. Still, it was nice to be treated as the customer for a change. I was far more used to the other side of the counter.

Eventually, she brought forth one of the biggest teapots I had ever seen. She struggled with the weight of it and held it in two hands with the use of a thick oven cloth. She deposited it down in the centre of the table with a grunt and a thump. Mrs Winchester immediately reached for it, no doubt some instinct from her usual role as tea pourer back at Oystercatcher Cottage. But Mrs Popkins' hand flashed out, quick as a snake, and rapped her smartly on the knuckles. 'Oh no you don't, my dear; you just leave that to steep. Can't have customers pouring their own tea in my shop. What would the vicar say?!'

My breath caught in my chest and I practically felt Mr Gout's do the same next to me.

We stared at Mrs Winchester, who in turn was staring at her still outreached hand as if it had just sprouted a dozen roses.

There'll be blood, I thought. *Mrs Winchester is going to murder the first person we've met and we'll be chased out of Morton-Upon-Mere by a mob of baying locals!*

But Mrs Winchester merely drew her hand back, offered the Tea Rooms proprietor a razor-thin smile, and said, 'Of course, *dear.*'

If Mrs Popkins noticed the significant drop in room temperature, she didn't show it. Instead, she beamed at us, then threw her hands up in the air, proclaimed, 'The scones!' and hurried off again, out of sight.

Mr Gout and I resumed our breathing.

'Well, isn't this cosy?' Mr Gout said in a slightly strained voice.

His housekeeper glowered. 'Delightful.'

Soon after, Mrs Popkins came scurrying back over with a platter piled high with the most delectable-looking scones I'd seen since leaving my parents' bakery. Any bad air there might have been disappeared with the steam, released as each was sliced open to receive its filling of cream and jam. There were lashings of each, and a slightly awkward moment was avoided, when I remembered, at the very last minute, where I was, and so spread on my cream first, before applying the jam. To do the reverse in Devon was almost as likely to have us chased out of town by an angry mob as was murder. At least, that's what I'd been told growing up. But Mrs Popkins' face as my knife hovered over the two dishes was proof enough for me.

This crisis averted, we enjoyed a most pleasurable luncheon. In fact, I don't believe I had seen my master so content in some weeks. But eventually, when the tea was drunk, and the scones reduced to mere crumbs on the empty platter (apart from three I had squirrelled away in a napkin on my lap for Klous), Mr Gout appeared to remember the real reason we were there.

'Mrs Popkins, you strike me as a person with some local knowledge,' he proclaimed as he dabbed at his mouth with a napkin and sat back in his chair. 'We're looking for a local property.'

'Well, I dare say I know most places hereabouts,' she replied. 'What's the name of the place?'

Mr Gout looked flummoxed. That curse really didn't want him to remember, did it?

'Castle Gout,' I supplied.

The change in our affable hostess was subtle but immediate.

'Oh?' she said, her smile taking on a slightly worried quality. 'Now what on earth would you be wanting with that old place? Ain't nothing up there but ruins and bad memories, or so they say.'

'But you know it? It's close by?' Mr Gout

could not keep the excitement out of his voice. His chubby face had split into a grin from ear to ear.

'Sure, it's close,' said Mrs Popkins, looking like she wished it weren't. ''Tis but a half-mile west of here. But there ain't been no Gouts in these parts for many a year. If you're hoping to meet–'

'There is now,' Mr Gout said with a bark of laughter.

I shot Mrs Winchester a nervous look. Was it wise, I wondered, letting that slip? But she simply shrugged.

Mrs Popkins' mouth had become an O of surprise. 'You don't mean to say *you're* a Gout?'

'Indeed I am!'

'Well, bless my soul! I never thought to see the day a Gout would come riding back into Morton-Upon-Mere. Not after all the tales I've heard...' she paused and looked guilty. 'Before my time, of course,' she said hurriedly. 'I only bought this place ten year back. But, you'll not go for long in this village without hearing the name Gout.'

'Is that so?' said Mr Gout, and he looked a little uncomfortable himself now. 'Of course I am but a distant relation. These tales...they are not too heinous, I hope?'

Mrs Popkins appeared to be getting over her shock. 'Oh, well,' she said, waving her oven cloth in the air as if to brush away his words. 'You know what gossips people are. Who can say what really happened all those years ago? All I know for sure is that the place has been abandoned for far longer than I've been living in these parts. There was some scandal or other, but...well, never mind all that!'

She bustled away, and did not return until we rose to leave. She took payment, smiled and waved us off, but I got the feeling that she was rather glad to see us gone.

#

'How long does it take to drink a cup o' tea!' Klous grumbled when he saw us coming out of the teahouse. He was sitting in the driver's seat of the wagon, dangling his stubby legs over the side. Custard had obviously awoken in our absence and was busily nibbling on the grass in the village square.

'You're supposed to be keeping out of sight!' Mrs Winchester said sharply, attempting to grab the rabbit. Custard simply hopped out of her reach and continued his impromptu dinner.

Klous waved a webbed hand at the deserted street. 'No one here t' see us, is there. I've seen more life in a ship's biscuit. Only person I've seen the whole time you've been gone was that poor woman you chased out of the teahouse.'

I assumed he meant Deirdre, the woman who had left quickly when we'd entered.

'What did she do when she left?' Mr Gout asked, raising a hand to his mouth, masking a small burp.

'Ran off. Often have that effect on women, do you?' the Klabautermann said, scowling. He was clearly upset at being left out on his own for so long, but his mood improved when I presented him with the three scones I'd saved.

'Now what?' Mrs Winchester asked.

'We head to the castle, surely?' I said.

Mr Gout nodded. 'Yes, I suppose so.'

'You suppose so?' said Mrs Winchester. 'You're about to set eyes on your childhood home for the first time in decades and that's all you have to say?'

Mr Gout gave an apologetic shrug. 'It's hard to know how I should feel about it. I've been searching for so long...'

'Well, we can't hang about here all day.'

'No,' Mr Gout agreed. 'Quite right. Let us see if we can find the place.'

#

We headed out of the village on the west road that Mrs Popkins had indicated. Morton-Upon-Mere was certainly not a large place, and it was hardly any time before the houses faltered, then stopped altogether. There was no other traffic on the road, the only sounds the rattling of our own wheels and the sharp, chattering cries of jackdaws that swooped low over the fields to our flanks as we passed.

After a few minutes, we reached a

turning on our right. A gated path, pitted with potholes and thick with grass down the middle, led off, bisecting the farmland, to where a rosy stone farmhouse could be seen in the distance. 'Ham Farm' had been painted in white letters on a flat-faced rock at the intersection of the main road and the path.

'Our friend Deirdre's abode, perhaps?' Mr Gout mused.

We carried on, and before long we came across another turning, this time to our left. Mr Gout pulled the cart in off the main road so we could inspect it in more detail. If Ham Farm's track had been in some disrepair, this one was in danger of being reclaimed by nature altogether. The only way it was discernible as a path at all was because there was a gap in the thick hedgerow that bordered the road. The track itself was almost lost beneath a thicket of brambles and grass. Patches of sandy gravel could be seen here and there, leading off toward a large copse of trees some eight hundred yards or so from the road. It was quite clear that no traffic had passed that way in some time. We might have disregarded it altogether, were it not for the small corner of a battered old wall sticking out of the undergrowth next to where Mr Gout had halted our wagon. There were letters, just visible, carved into the stone in deep, weathered lines. It wasn't clear, but I thought I could make out A, T, and a G.

'Is this it, do you think?' asked Mrs

Winchester, flaring her nostrils in obvious distaste.

I turned to my master. 'Does it look familiar at all?'

He grimaced, rubbing at a spot between his eyes with two porky fingers. 'I fear I could sit right on top of it and I wouldn't know.'

'Well, we're not getting the horse through this lot,' Klous declared.

I looked at the thick brambles. He wasn't wrong. If this was indeed Castle Gout, then we'd have to try to reach it on foot first. The track would need some serious clearing before any vehicle would get through. 'I think we should check it out,' I said anyway.

Mr Gout, however, looked reluctant. He glanced over his shoulder, back towards the village. 'Maybe we could get a room for the night at The Wild Garlic.'

'I can't abide garlic,' Mrs Winchester said, as if that somehow ruled out the possibility.

'We can't stop now,' I insisted. 'Not after we've come all this way. It's just a few brambles.'

'Easy for you to say. They're head height for me!' said Klous. Custard had already hopped back inside Mrs Winchester's bag, clearly having no intention of walking anywhere.

'I'll give you a piggyback,' I offered.

The Klabautermann gave me an offended look. 'Like a *child*?'

'Suit yourself,' I said. 'Come on!'

And I set off, not looking back to see if the others would follow. I stamped down the brambles with my boots as best I could. It was slow going, but the track was passable with a little effort. I heard some hushed bickering behind me, but paid it no heed.

I couldn't say exactly why I felt so insistent that we not turn back. It just felt wrong to me, somehow. We had to reach the castle, as soon as possible. It felt important. I was sure that if we could just get Mr Gout within eyesight of the place, it would force some memories to return. He had remembered other parts of his life, after all. If he could just *see* his former home, I felt sure that things would get easier. We could stay at the Wild Garlic for a month and be no closer to progress on breaking his curse. Plus, there were the residents to worry about. Despite my master's feigned lack of concern, I knew he must also realise the dangers they might pose to us. We had no way of knowing what happened here. No way of knowing exactly how popular, or more importantly *unpopular,* his sudden reappearance might be. Mrs Popkins certainly hadn't seemed comfortable with the knowledge that he was a Gout, and she was a relative newcomer to the area. Deirdre had practically fled at the sight of him.

No. We needed answers, and I felt sure we would only find them in one place. There had to be a reason whoever cursed Mr Gout had made him forget his home. They wanted him to feel...

what? Lost? Alone? It had to be deliberate. That, coupled with making him unable to sleep under a solid roof, had me convinced that the spell caster wanted to cut Mr Gout off from the person he had been before.

The only question was: why?

I had to admit to myself that part of my excitement in finding Castle Gout was due to my own intense interest in discovering more about my master. Ever since I'd met the man, I had felt like I was only ever getting the slimmest glimpse of who he truly was. I hoped the discovery of his childhood home would change that.

'Ow!'

Lost in my own thoughts, it made me start when a particularly vicious bramble dragged across my leg as I tried to push my way through. I was forced to pause and detach it from where it now snagged on my dress. Klous appeared at my side.

'What's the matter, miss? It's just a few brambles.' He stuck his enormous tongue out at me and moved past in a giant bound.

'Oh, grow up!' I called after him.

A flash of movement caught my attention, and I turned to see a pair of eyes looking out at me from the undergrowth. They were human eyes, green, but I'm not sure if that was a comfort or not. When they met mine, I gave a little start and the eyes widened. A figure was visible for a split second, rushing away from us through the long grasses.

'I've just seen a boy in the undergrowth,' I said.

Klous looked at me strangely. 'Is this a puberty thing?' he asked, doubtfully.

'What? No! I mean that I literally just saw a boy watching us from the hedge.'

'Oh...' Klous shrugged. 'Well, it's probably just a curious villager.'

'I'm going to follow him,' I said.

Klous put his little clawed hands on his hips. 'Sounds like a pubery thing to me,' he mumbled as I started to wade my way through the brambles in the direction the boy had taken. I chose to ignore the Kobold.

It was even more hard going off what little was left of the path, and although Klous was quickly lost to sight, I wasn't making very fast progress. But I kept pushing on, something in my gut telling me that the face I'd briefly seen might be important. When looking for a big cursed house, I reasoned, it was important to note anybody hanging around. Even feral-looking boys in bushes.

I was just starting to think I'd lost him, when I stumbled into a little clearing amid prickly thorns and I found him, crouched down on his hands and feet like a frog. He bared his teeth at me, looking ready to spring.

Now, I don't know about you, but I was certainly not used to strange boys baring their teeth at me. He looked to be about my age, although it was hard to tell how tall he might be from his current position. His skin looked darkened by the sun, as happens when someone spends all their time outdoors, and judging by the state of his ragged clothes, a good portion of them might have been dirt. He had sandy-coloured hair that fell down his back in a jumbled tangle. His eyes were a startling green.

'Um…good afternoon,' I said.

I was startled. I'm not sure exactly what would have been a more suitable thing to say to someone in the circumstances, but 'good morning' was the first thing that came to mind.

The boy looked equally at a loss. There was something of a startled alley cat about his features. He seemed even more surprised to see me than I was to see him.

Then he hissed at me.

He actually hissed at me. Like a cat.

One of my eyebrows quirked up and I was almost surprised to hear myself say, 'Well, is that a polite thing to say to a stranger?'

Perhaps I should have been more scared. But the more I looked at the boy, the more he seemed like a vulnerable animal. Of course, a cornered beast can be the most vicious of all.

'My friends are just over there,' I said, gesturing vaguely.

'Leave!' the boy croaked. His voice was cracked and rasped, as if he hadn't used it in some time.

'What?'

'Leave this place!' He said it in a sort of snarl, making him look even more feline.

'Look, I don't know who you think I am...' I began, but the boy didn't give me a chance to finish. He sprang to his feet and, although he made no motion actually towards me, I found myself stepping back in shock.

'Just go!' he spat. 'Take your weird friends and get out of here!'

With that, he spun on his heel and disappeared into the undergrowth.

PART THREE

I stood for a moment, staring after the boy. What was going on here? I had spent no small amount of time thinking about what we might find at Castle Gout, but in all my wonderings I had never expected to find...well, a person. I expected monsters, phantoms, witches, sorcerers...any number of supernatural entities. But not a normal boy. Alright, he hadn't exactly been normal. Frankly, he looked half feral, but still. It never occurred to me that there might be someone actually living on the property. I couldn't say for sure, but I was willing to wager that's what the strange boy was doing.

The only other question was: Why did he want us to leave so badly?

I made my way back to the path to a concerned-looking Klous.

'Where did you run off to?' he asked accusingly.

'I found the boy,' I said.

'Oh, so there actually was one, then?'

'Yes,' I said, nettled. 'I told you there was.'

'Well?'

'Well, what?'

'Well, what did he want?'

'He told me we should leave. He was quite insistent about it, actually. Then he ran off.'

Klous looked even less happy than before. 'Perfect. Not ominous at all.'

I sighed. 'Come on. The others are catching us up.'

I looked back. Mrs Winchester and Mr Gout were following. I tried to smother a small laugh. Mrs Winchester had lifted her skirts up above her knees, and was tiptoeing through the trampled undergrowth I had left behind, her nostrils so widely flared they looked like two great Os in her face. Mr Gout, on the other hand, had adopted a sort of springing jump from one delicate foot to the other. Every time he jumped, he made a little 'Hup!' noise.

'What are you sniggering at?' Mrs Winchester demanded, as she eventually drew close enough to make out my expression. 'This was your stupid idea.'

I turned away and followed Klous, not daring to comment for fear I would burst out laughing.

To be fair, the going was harder than I had initially imagined. The overgrown undergrowth did not let up. Some fairly sizeable saplings had even sprung up in places. Every now and again, one or another of us would let out a muffled curse as a foot got caught in brambles or slipped into the ruts still left by wagons long ago. But after twenty minutes or so, things finally opened out a little. The track got wider, less choked with weeds, and we could walk almost normally. However, there had not been a single sign that we were heading towards anything particular.

'Are we sure we're going the right way?' Klous grumbled.

'Does anything look familiar?' Mrs Winchester asked Mr Gout, but he wiped his sweat-slick brow and shook his head.

'Apart from the fact that I could have sworn this exact bedevilled stinging nettle stung me five minutes ago, no, I'm afraid not.'

'Let's keep going,' I insisted. 'This has to lead somewhere!'

'Everywhere leads somewhere, girl,' Mrs Winchester snapped, sucking at her thumb where a bramble had caught it. 'The question is, is it somewhere we want to be?'

Luckily for me, I was proven right just a couple of minutes later.

Castle Gout appeared from round a bend in the track. Of course, technically, it could have been any building, but I just knew it was what we were looking for.

The four of us stumbled to a halt and stared.

'Gosh,' said Klous.

'My word,' said Mr Gout.

'Well, bugger me!' said Mrs Winchester.

It was a huge gothic mansion.

The track we had been following ran into a large, flat area of gravel, presumably once designed to give expensive carriages an uninterrupted view of the exercise in extravagance laid out before them. This courtyard, much like the track that led to it, had not been spared the ravages of time, however. It was no longer a sea of grey gravel, but more an archipelago of weed islands. A few small trees had even taken root in the once sterile space.

The house was still imposing, however. Two enormous towers, complete with pointed conical roofs, reached for the sky on either side of the grandest building I had ever seen. I tried to count the windows, but my eyes skipped from one intricately carved stone frame to another, and I gave up. I thought there must have been at least four floors. The central doorway was one massive arch. The stone was carved so densely with motifs and images that it was almost hard to look at; from this distance I could not make out a single defining feature, save for a giant boar's head at the crest of the arch. The doors themselves were made of ancient-looking timber blackened and hardened with age so that it gave the impression of being stronger than steel. They were reached by a set of stone steps to either side that swept up in to a square landing, lined with swirling balustrades. The eerie effect was only added to by the fact that, from ground to roof, the entire building seemed wrapped in brown vines, like a wisteria gone mad.

The four of us stared for some minutes. I remembered seeing Oystercatcher Cottage for the first time; how I had been surprised to find the larger-than-life Mr Gout living in such a humble place. But this was grander than anything I could have imagined, even in those early days of our acquaintance.

Klous was the first to break the silence.

'Just how rich was your family?' he asked – a question that I had been thinking myself and imagined Mrs Winchester must have been too.

'Quite rich, it would seem,' was Mr Gout's muttered reply. He sounded as though his thoughts were a thousand miles away. Or perhaps, more accurately, a few decades away.

'Should we…go inside?' I suggested.

'Well, we have come all this way,' said Mrs Winchester.

No one moved.

'Does it seem familiar, Theo?' Mrs Winchester asked after a few more moments of silence.

Mr Gout scratched his chins. 'Hard to say,' he said. 'I keep thinking it might seem familiar, but then I start to feel groggy and have to look away.'

'The curse, no doubt.'

'Yes. Perhaps we should take this slowly. Let's try getting a little closer.'

The gravel crunched under our feet as we

approached the towering mansion. It loomed over us like a storm-cloud.

'Cheery place,' Klous observed.

'I suppose it was bound to look a little… delapidated. It has been abandoned for some considerable time,' said Mr Gout.

'Can't think why,' Klous muttered.

We walked up to the foot of the right-hand set of stairs and halted.

'How do you feel now?' I asked, craning my neck back to look up at the building.

'Like I have a hangover I don't deserve,' Mr Gout grunted, wiping a hand down his face and reaching out towards the stonework to steady himself.

The effect was immediate.

The second his hand made contact with the stone, he went stiff, then tore it away and cried out in pain. He clutched his head with both hands as if he feared it might explode, took two staggering steps, then fell to the ground.

'Theo!' Mrs Winchester was by his side in a flash.

I hurriedly joined her, the gravel digging painfully into my knees as I knelt. 'Is he alright?'

'Does he look alright?' she snapped. 'Theo? Come on, you great lout, stop fooling around!'

But there was no response. Mr Gout was out cold.

'What the bleedin 'ell happened?' Klous cried, jumping up and down in agitation.

'It was when he touched the stone,' I said. 'It must be the curse!'

Custard, who had been riding in Mrs Winchester's bag, had now hopped to the ground and was worriedly nuzzling his master's face.

To my immense relief, Mr Gout groaned and started trying to sit up.

'Easy now,' Mrs Winchester said, fussing around him like a fly around an elephant. 'Take it slow. You had a nasty fall there.'

'I...I'm alright,' he said groggily. 'Not sure what happened. My word, my *head.*'

Between us, we got him standing again. He swayed a little, but seemed to be recovering fast.

'Clearly the curse isn't keen on you going home,' I observed.

He gave a weak smile. 'So it would seem. But I think it was a one-off. Just a build-up of tensions. I'm feeling better by the second. In fact...yes. I can look at the place without going cross-eyed now.'

He gazed up at the expansive building before us, reached out a tentative hand, then grasped the stonework again. There was a collective intake of breath, but, although he wobbled alarmingly, Mr Gout remained standing. He closed his eyes.

'What's happening?' Mrs Winchester asked. 'What do you see?'

'I'm not sure,' Mr Gout said, eyes still closed. 'It is...confusing. There are a great many images, but all jumbled up. I...I think...I need...'

'What? What do you need?' I asked.

He removed his hand from the stone and reopened his eyes. 'I need a cup of tea. And some lunch.'

'You just ate, you great glutton!' Mrs Winchester snapped.

'The scones? That was just a snack,' he complained.

I relaxed. He was clearly feeling much better.

'Should we try to go in?' Klous asked. He was looking up at the castle with wide eyes.

'Is that wise?' I asked. I thought that if the merest touch of stone had caused Mr Gout to faint, then actually entering the building could be dangerous indeed.

But my master nodded. 'Yes. I am prepared now. We must gain entry.'

Even so, the foot he placed on the bottom step was tentative, and we all held our breath yet again. But after a slight pause, he simply nodded again and continued his ascent. We followed. I felt nervous touching the fabric of the building myself, despite knowing that the curse was Mr Gout's alone. Still, we reached the top of the stairs without further incident.

We came out onto a wide landing before an enormous set of double wooden doors. I reached them last and found the others staring. I looked.

Painted across the door, in startling green, was a large lily.

'Well now, this is interesting,' said my master, scratching his chin.

'It's the sigil!' I burst out. 'Does that mean…'

'I am not sure what it means. But we must be careful. If this curse was placed on me by the very same being who has dogged our recent cases, then we must expect danger.'

My mind whirled. What did this mean? The green lily. This meant that, whatever had happened to Mr Gout all those years ago was done by the very same person who created the Alp who preyed on my granny. The same person who sent a curse-carrying Zombie to Abermwyl.

They were all connected. That couldn't be a coincidence.

Mr Gout reached out a hand to try the door, but I grabbed at it on instinct.

'Let me,' I insisted.

Mr Gout smiled. 'Yes, I suppose that makes sense. Perhaps it would be best.'

Hesitating only slightly to wonder what horrible curse the being behind the green lily might have placed on the front door, I reached out and placed my hand against it.

Nothing happened.

Then, to my surprise, it gave way under the slight pressure I was applying and moved inwards. It creaked ominously. It gave a long, loud, drawn-out groan that almost had me scampering back down the steps. Inside, all was in darkness.

'Well, that's reassuring,' said Klous.

'It wasn't even locked,' I said. 'That seems odd.'

'Odd? It's an abandoned stately home in the middle of nowhere, covered in vines and vandalised with powerful magic sigils,' said Mrs Winchester, peering over my shoulder into the depths of the building. 'Odd doesn't really cover it.'

Nothing large, hairy, or slimy rushed out at us, so I pushed the door all the way open. A little daylight filtered past us into the cavernous entrance hall. It was odd. At this time of day, the light should have easily illuminated the space, yet it barely made an impact. It was just powerful enough to trace the vague outline of a structure directly in front of us. Stone carvings peered out of the shadows from the ceiling. Disturbingly, no matter how hard I looked, I couldn't make out what any of them were. There was the suggestion of a face here, the hint of a wing there, something scaly off to the left, something with claws to the right. It was unsettling.

'Nice place you've got,' said Klous.

'Do you think it's safe to go in?' I asked.

'Are we sure we *want* to go in?' asked Mrs Winchester.

It was a moment before Mr Gout answered. 'Yes,' he said. 'To both questions. We have to know what is inside and, as far as I can tell, it should be safe. To all of you, at any rate. Truthfully, I cannot predict how I might be affected. We shall have to be on our toes.'

'Shouldn't we...I don't know, *prepare* or something?' I said.

Mr Gout gave a humourless chuckle. 'My dear Clementine, this curse has plagued me for longer than I care to say. Certainly longer than you yourself have been alive. In all that time, I have learnt exactly nothing about it. Until just now, I had not the slightest inkling who had cast it. Even now, all I know is that we have come across their handiwork before. I have had no defence against it. No counter to its powers. Should I *try* to prepare against whatever it might have in store for me next, I really couldn't say what I would do.'

'We beat their last curse,' I said. 'The one the Zombie bought.'

'Ah yes,' he said. 'Although forgive me, but as I recall, we should both of us have perished at its hands had it not been for a certain deceased rabbit of mine.'

'We saved the village!' I protested.

'That much is true,' he admitted. 'And in that spirit, there is one thing I can think of to do.'

'What?' asked Mrs Winchester.

Mr Gout looked straight ahead into the shadowy interior of his former home and grinned. 'Go first!' he said, and stepped sharply over the threshold.

PART FOUR

Nothing happened.

Mr Gout stood just inside the doorway, bouncing up and down on the balls of his feet, while nothing continued to happen.

'Now what?' said Klous.

'I haven't the foggiest,' said Mr Gout. 'But I have not dropped dead yet. I can detect no obvious signs of anything untoward.'

'Apart from this entire building, you mean,' Klous grumbled, but he bounced through the doorway anyway. I followed and heard Mrs Winchester's hesitant footsteps behind me.

'Well, it's big, Theo. I'll give you that,' she said. 'But I think I prefer Oystercatcher Cottage myself.'

'A thoroughly superior residence, my dear,' he agreed. 'Well, it would seem the house does not abhor my presence quite so much as I had first feared.' He walked forward into the darkness.

I followed, slowly, expecting something horrible to come leaping out at us from the many dark corners of the room. But nothing did, so we looked around.

It was still very hard to see. The unnatural darkness persisted, and nothing seemed to come into focus until you were practically on top of it. I found this out by nearly walking into a sideboard.

It was not particularly impressive, as sideboards go. It was large, made of dark wood, and holding only a single glass vase filled with desiccated flowers. It looked as though they had simply been left there; as if someone had walked out the door one day and never returned to tidy them up. That was quite possibly what had happened.

Then I heard a sound.

It was the softest thing, almost nothing. The slightest tread on a wooden floor.

I heard it again, a little louder.

'Um...we're not expecting anyone to actually be here, are we?' I asked, thinking of the boy.

Mr Gout was by my side in a second. 'What is it?'

I didn't answer, because at that moment a small black cat trotted out of the shadows towards us.

It meowed at us, in the expectant way of all cats.

I let out a breath and almost laughed. 'It's

just a cat,' I said, stating the obvious. I turned to my master to share the joke, only to find him frozen, staring at the creature as if he had seen the devil itself. The cat approached him, and my master executed such a leap from a standing start that for a moment I thought he had been physically hurled across the room. The cat hissed at the sudden movement, backing away.

Then I realised what had so shaken my master.

He'd told me, just a few short weeks ago as our wagon left the Thicklewood estate, that he'd had a brother. A brother who had died in dire circumstances. A brother who had returned as a revenant.

In the form of a cat.

I found myself backing away from the startled creature, but then Mr Gout spoke.

'It's alright...it's alright. It's just a cat.' He looked calmer; amused, even.

'Are you sure?'

He removed his pocket square from the breast pocket of his jacket and used it to wipe the perspiration from his forehead, then chuckled. 'Quite sure. My apologies, Clementine, my dear. I suppose, what with being back here, I have Matthias on my mind.'

'Your brother?' said Mrs Winchester, who had been attracted over by the commotion along with Klous. She looked decidedly unhappy. 'He's not here, surely? You said you...' she paused, uncertain how to finish the sentence.

'He's not here,' Mr Gout assured. 'He has long since passed on. The cat just...well, it took me by surprise. It doesn't even look that much like Matthias, now I examine it properly. My apologies, everyone.'

'What's it doing here, do you think?' Klous asked, eyeing the creature, which was now ignoring us and had begun to wash itself.

'Hunting mice, I expect,' Mrs Winchester said, looking into the shadows that surrounded us with distaste. 'I bet this place is riddled with 'em. Rats, too!'

'It is peculiar,' Mr Gout admitted, scratching at his chin and giving the apparently unconcerned cat a critical look. 'There is potent magic at work in this place. I hadn't thought to find anything living inside. Perhaps you were right about the boy after all, Miss Trussel.'

The cat did seem in good condition. Perhaps the boy I'd seen was looking after it?

Then I noticed another quiet thought tickling the back of my mind. It was like that feeling you get when people say someone is walking over your grave. I shivered and felt the irresistible urge to turn my head.

There was something wrong with the door at the end of the corridor. I couldn't tell what it was, but I knew that there was something. It looked like all the other doors we'd seen, so far as I could tell. Dark mahogany, but faded through years of neglect, the shine gone from the wood. The only difference was that we'd found most doors closed, whereas this one was slightly ajar. Only just – so little that I almost didn't notice – but open nonetheless.

The cat wouldn't go near it. That should have been our first warning sign. As I made my way down the corridor towards it the cat let out a long, mournful meowing. That should have been our second warning sign. It began to brush up against my legs as I walked, then almost tripped me, cutting in front of my feet so that I had to hitch my stride and stumbled.

'What is the matter with you?' I paused and bent down to scratch the thing beneath the chin, but it darted away from me again, out of reach. I tutted. 'Well, *fine*, but you came to me.'

I stood up in time to see Mr Gout, who had overtaken me, place a hand upon the door and gently push it open. At the same time, something caught his eye on the floorboards at his feet. 'Huh…' he said, which is when it happened.

Something grabbed the door from behind and pulled it fully open with such speed that it hit the wall with a sharp crack that rang out around us like a gunshot. I caught a flash of movement from beyond the door and Mr Gout was sent flying with a cry. He landed on his back ten feet from the door.

'What–' Mrs Winchester managed, before something long and whiplike erupted from the shadows beyond the door, hit her in the chest and forced her up against the corridor wall, pinning her in place.

Klous made a strange sound, somewhere between a shout of surprise and a croak, then sprang backwards, doing an awkward midair cartwheel to avoid another long shape that had shot out towards him from the open door. Custard had appeared on the floor, spinning in circles like an excited dog, teeth bared.

I made a move towards Mr Gout, who now seemed to be inexplicably sliding across the floorboards towards the door, but I had made barely a step in his direction when something slithered around my ankle and yanked, hard. I yelped as I was pulled from my feet, coming down awkwardly, one arm pinned beneath me. Whatever had my ankle did not let go, and I felt a flare of pain, little spikes in a ring, as if I'd been bitten. Then I too was dragged towards the open doorway. I glimpsed my attacker through the tangle of my hair. There was something that looked like a thick green rope wrapped tightly around my left ankle. It disappeared in a taut line through the open doorway.

I clawed at the hair covering my face to get a better view.

Whatever had me was latched on to Mr Gout and Mrs Winchester, too. Both were struggling against its pull towards the door. Custard jumped up onto my chest and headbutted me anxiously in the face.

I tried to sit up but was immediately thrown onto my back again, hitting my head on the floor, as there was another sharp tug from whatever held me. Blinking back stars and tears, I tried to focus on my foot as I was dragged, inch by inch, towards the waiting doorway, the dead rabbit fidgeting nervously on my chest. Desperately, I reached for the thing wrapped around my ankle, but it was useless. Every time I got close, there was another tug and I would fall back prostrate again. The pain in my ankle was increasing. My foot felt cold, as though it were wrapped in bands of iron. I became aware of a powerful smell that was filling the hallway; a thick, rotten vegetation stink. I could almost feel the heat of it, as though I'd stuck my face into a compost heap.

Help came in the form of Klous.

Being nimbler than the rest of us, it seemed he had avoided our attacker. He bounded into my vision and, with a flash of his clawed hand, stabbed a small knife into the rope that held me. I felt the thing spasm, then the tight hold on my ankle released. Something shot back into the darkness.

'Thanks!' I gasped, pushing Custard gently aside, scrambling to a kneeling position and then to my feet.

I got my first clear look at what was attacking us.

The things I had taken for green rope were in fact...well, I wasn't sure. But they weren't rope. They looked organic. Alive. Like slithering green tentacles. One still had a firm hold around Mrs Winchester and, although she had remained standing, she was being dragged inexorably towards the doorway, one halting step at a time.

Mr Gout seemed out cold. He lay completely still, held by at least three of the tentacles, which pulled at his bulk with a creeping, eager hunger.

'Don't just stare, girl, *do something*!' Mrs Winchester cried, beating at the thing that held her, to little effect.

At her words, I snapped out of my shock, just in time, as it turned out, to spring away from another of the tentacles as it shot out towards me. Klous bounced up beside me.

'Grab her!'

I did as he asked, coming up behind the struggling housekeeper and wrapping my arm around her chest. I grasped at the thing that held her and yelped in pain as what felt like a thousand tiny needles dug into my palms. I gritted my teeth and held on, attempting to counter the force that was forever pulling her closer to the waiting door.

It was little use: I was just being pulled along with her, but then Klous was there again, springing up to the taut line emanating from Mrs Winchester's chest and swiping, cutting it clean through with his knife. There was a loud *snap*, and I fell backwards to the floor once more, this time with Mrs Winchester on top of me.

'Get off me, you daft girl!' she cried,

struggling out of the now loose bonds. I might have pointed out I had come off far worse than she, but the impact had driven the air from my lungs and all I could manage was indignant spluttering.

We got to our feet with the minimum amount of kicking and shoving possible. Klous had already bounced over to where the prostrate Mr Gout was still sliding ever forward along the floor. The spiky tentacles were wrapped tightly around his body and I winced in sympathy. My ankle and hands were throbbing painfully from where they had come in contact with the things.

Klous was having more difficulty freeing my master than he'd had with us. Whatever was controlling the tentacles seemed to have wisened to his attacks, and was flinging tentacle after tentacle at him, meaning he had to bob and weave, jump and hop, just to stay ahead of them.

He needed help.

With unspoken communication, Mrs Winchester and I surged forward. Though not as nimble as our Kobold friend, we managed to dodge the thrashing green limbs that came for us, and we reached Mr Gout's side. I was just contemplating trying to wrench his bonds off with my already injured hands when Klous yelled '*Catch!*' and his little knife skittered across the floorboards towards me. I snatched it up, and between us, Mrs Winchester and I managed to free Mr Gout. But we were still under attack. I yelped at a stinging bite to my shoulder and turned my head to find yet another tentacle attempting to slither around my neck. I twirled away and lashed out with Klous's blade.

'We have to get away!' Mrs Winchester cried, tugging with all her might on Mr Gout's arm, attempting to drag him back up the hallway. Her efforts were having little success, however, and I hurried to help, grabbing his other arm and heaving.

But this left us both defenceless, and the tentacles were soon upon us again. I was starting to panic.

'*Get down!*' Klous bellowed. The little creature had dropped to the floor and was kneeling, facing the open door. I had no idea what he intended to do, but when I saw his throat quiver, then swell, I dropped to the ground and covered my head. Through my hands, I watched as a large sack around his throat inflated like a toad.

Then he vomited a fireball through the doorway.

I am not sure how else to put it. A ball of spinning green flame erupted from his gaping jaws and flew down the corridor. It cast flickering emerald shadows on the walls as it passed and then, just for a moment, it illuminated a whole knot of writhing, snake-like appendages, before crashing into whatever it was with a sizzle like onions hitting a hot pan.

The tentacles immediately stopped their attack and writhed and thrashed, hitting the walls and ceiling in their haste to retreat back to...what?

We didn't want to hang around to find out. But Mr Gout was still out cold.

'We should get him out,' Klous said urgently, bouncing up and down. 'If this is the curse, we should get him as far away from the castle as we can!'

'And how do you suppose we do that?' snapped Mrs Winchester.

She had a point. Mr Gout was not a small man. Even with the three of us, I couldn't see us getting him far.

'Well, we have to do something!' I cried, tears pricking at my eyes as foam started to froth at Mr Gout's mouth.

Mrs Winchester swore. 'Come on, girl, grab a leg and pull!'

I did so. I pulled with all my might, terror lending me strength, and, somehow, between the two of us, we got him sliding across the floor towards the front door. It was not a dignified exit. But the closer to the opening we got, the smaller the tremors that wracked his unconscious body became, which made us pull all the harder. Klous bounced around us like a demented frog, shouting out encouragement.

'Pull! Pull! Come on, put your backs into it!'

'You could do something to help instead of all this caterwauling!' Mrs Winchester shouted, her face red from exertion.

'I am many things, you old crone,' Klous

said, nose in the air. 'But none of 'em is built to be tugging around great fat men by their ankles.'

'Useless,' Mrs Winchester muttered as we hauled Mr Gout's feet back out into the sunshine. Klous did at least grab the frantic Custard, who had been headbutting his unconscious master's side with increasing ferocity, and heartbreakingly clear anxiety.

The effect was immediate, although it took us a moment to notice. Mr Gout began to awaken the moment just the tiniest part of him was removed from the castle's interior. Unfortunately, this resulted in him giving a particularly vigorous kick with the leg that Mrs Winchester was pulling on. It caught her under the chin, making her lose her grip and subsequently shoot over backwards into the balustrade.

She swore till she was practically blue in the face, calling Mr Gout, and Klous, virtually every name under the sun, all while clutching at her jaw and struggling to get back to her feet. Klous had the good grace to remain silent, while I was simply glad not to be included in her tirade. Mr Gout began to stir for real. The convulsions had stopped, but he still flopped around on the ground, groaning, half in and half out of the doorway. This only seemed to spur his housekeeper on to fresh remonstrations, and her language became so colourful I blushed.

'Such language!'

The voice stopped Mrs Winchester dead

mid-syllable. Klous leapt over Mr Gout's prostrate form and onto the balustrade in alarm. I whipped my head around in the direction from which it had come.

Deirdre, the woman from the tea shop, was standing in the gravel at the bottom of the steps. She looked angry.

'I knew you were no good,' she declared. 'From the moment I clapped eyes on you. How could you be, when you came dragging that terrible man back in to Morton-Upon-Mere?'

'What's that?' Mrs Winchester snapped at her, recovering from her shock with admirable speed, although still massaging her wounded jaw. 'It's rude to sneak up on people!'

The woman ignored her, her eyes wide.

'After all these years,' she said. 'And he walks into Morton-Upon-Mere like he never left!'

'You recognise this man?' I asked, wary. Mr Gout was still coming to at my feet.

She snorted. 'I should say I do. He ruined my life.'

Mrs Winchester glared at the woman. 'Mr Gout has never ruined anybody's life!'

Deirdre didn't reply, just kept staring up at the stirring Mr Gout. She was wringing her hands.

I became aware that Klous was attempting to hide behind a gargoyle.

'I think she's already seen you,' I said, not unkindly. He made silent shushing motions at me.

'I have,' the woman confirmed, but she made

no further comment. If she was at all shocked at Klous's unusual appearance, she didn't show it. She had eyes only for Mr Gout.

'Did you do this?' Mrs Winchester asked, pointing at Mr Gout where he lay.

At that, the woman finally came out of her trance, bristling. 'How dare you? You come back here with that...that *man,* and you accuse *me* of hurting *him*? It's obviously the curse that's got him!'

'We're not accusing anyone of anything,' I blurted.

'Well, he's the one on the floor, not you,' Mrs Winchester pointed out, glaring daggers at the woman.

'You said it was the curse,' I prompted. 'What do you know about that?'

The woman looked at me coldly. 'I know it ruined my life!'

'Very well,' I said slowly, trying to be reasonable. This woman clearly knew something important. 'If that's true, then Mr Gout is not your enemy. He is a victim of the curse. He didn't cast it.'

'You think that makes a difference?' she said. 'You think that makes a difference at all? He might not have cast the curse, but he's the reason for it. He's the reason my Archie...' She snapped her mouth closed, as if she'd said too much.

'Archie? Is that...your husband?' I guessed.

Her mouth tightened. 'I don't have to answer your questions.'

'If you won't answer Clementine's, then you can answer mine,' Mrs Winchester said. 'Only I ain't so polite.'

She advanced towards the woman with a grim expression.

Deirdre took a step back. 'You stay away from me!' she cried.

'Not until you tell me what is going on in that mansion!'

At first, I thought the woman would refuse to answer again. Her face was cold and stiff as she glared at my still half-conscious master. But eventually she spoke, and her voice was tired and sad. 'He tried to go home. The curse don't like that.'

'And what would you know about it?' Mrs Winchester demanded. 'I warn you, if you don't tell me right now, I'll set this Kobold on you!'

'Oi!' Klous looked scandalised. 'I ain't attacking no one. Not unless I wants to, at any rate.'

Deirdre looked at him properly for the first time. 'You're a Kobold, are you?'

'A Klabautermann, technically,' he replied with a sniff.

'That's supposed to mean something to me, is it?'

Klous's bulbous eyes narrowed. 'Ignorant humans,' he grumbled, then turned his back on the woman, jumping back down by Mr Gout's side.

'The curse?' Mrs Winchester prompted, taking another step forward. 'What do you know about it?'

'That's what I should be asking you!' the woman spat, pointing a crooked finger at us. 'You show up here, out of the blue, with none other than Theophilius Gout at your side, after all this time!'

There came a low groan. Mr Gout was waking.

'Look, this isn't getting us anywhere,' I said. 'It's obvious that we both have questions. We promise to answer yours if you answer ours. What do you say?'

She took some time to reply.

'Fine,' she said eventually. 'But not here. Not by that…that place.' She nodded at the castle looming over us. Mr Gout groaned again, and she looked down at him. 'You can bring him to the farm. I can help.' Her eyes moved to Mrs Winchester. 'But this doesn't mean I like you!'

'I'll try to bear the disappointment,' the housekeeper said through clenched teeth.

PART FIVE

Deirdre's farm turned out to be Ham Farm, the one we had passed on the road earlier in the day, and Deirdre herself turned out to be Mrs Ham. It was a struggle to get Mr Gout there, but once he came around for real, it became easier. Mrs Winchester helped me get him back to the cart, then she took the reins. Mrs Ham came with us, sitting on the very edge of the wagon with her nose in the air as if every inch of her person that touched it was an affront to her respectability. I tried to get her into conversation, but she would not be drawn, merely stating, 'This is the one,' when we reached the correct turning.

The track to the farm was in far better repair than the one to Castle Gout had been. No brambles or undergrowth impeded our progress, and the larger potholes had been filled with gravel and stone fairly recently. We drove alongside a field of sandy-coloured cattle who watched us pass mournfully, mouths chewing, tails swishing.

'Is your farm dairy or beef?' I asked, trying again to win the woman over. She didn't answer.

We pulled up under a large beech tree that in summer would have offered much shade to a well-swept farmyard. The farmhouse sat opposite, a squat but pleasant rose-coloured stone building, which, on further inspection, was in dire need of repairs. The window frames looked rotten. The roof was covered in moss and missing several tiles. Even the paint on the front door was peeling. Although the two buildings could not have looked more different, there was something about the place that reminded me of Castle Gout. I pondered over that as we helped Mr Gout down. It was the quiet, I realised. I knew farms from back home. They were busy places, always something going on. But here there was nothing. A stillness hung over the farm, just like it had Mr Gout's former home.

'Is your husband home?' I asked.

I was rewarded with a sharp look and an announcement from Mrs Ham. 'I'll make some tea. You're not to come inside. You can wait over there.' She gestured to an old picnic bench set up in a patch of overgrown grass to one side of the yard. 'Don't wander,' she added, with a stern look Mrs Winchester would have been proud to call her own.

As it was, the housekeeper merely sniffed and said, 'Wouldn't dream of it.'

I, however, found it a hard order to obey.

I was desperate to look around the farm. There were answers here, I was sure of it. I couldn't really have said why, but it was obvious Mrs Ham knew more than she was saying, and if she persisted in being difficult, then we would just have to find answers elsewhere.

'I'm going to look around.'

'Well, ain't you the little rebel?' Klous said with a smirk.

Mrs Winchester raised one eyebrow, then gave a small nod. This was practically a glowing endorsement. Mr Gout was still looking fairly stunned. He sat, staring into the middle distance, with Custard curled up on his lap.

I wandered off in no particular direction. I didn't really know what I was looking for. I found myself drawn to the left of the building, where some ancient piece of farm machinery had been left to gently rot in a patch of two-foot-tall grass. I had no idea what it was once supposed to have been. It was like everything else in the place; run down, almost forgotten. I admit it seemed to me at odds with Mrs Ham's personality. I barely knew her, of course, but she seemed to me very much in the Mrs Winchester mould. I imagined she took fierce pride in cleanliness. The farm wasn't dirty, exactly. There was a little dust, of course, but it hadn't rained in a while and no amount of sweeping could keep dust from a farmyard. Things nevertheless seemed neglected, as if they had simply been left to fall apart. Something told me, however, that if I were to gain access to the farmhouse, I would find a dresser full of brightly polished china, and a linen cupboard stuffed with spotless, neatly pressed linen. Mrs Ham was certainly no slouch, I mused, but she was just one woman. There was a lot to do on a farm. More than one person could manage, no matter how hard they might try. Where, I wondered, was Mr Ham?

I continued down the side of the building. I didn't want to get too close to the house, in case Mrs Ham happened to look out and see me through the window. I might have been brave enough to go poking about when she had specifically forbad me to do any such thing, but that didn't mean I relished the idea of getting caught. I'd just see what was behind the farmhouse, then rejoin the others.

What I found stopped me in my tracks.

There was a large patch of lawn onto which the house looked out. Beyond it was a fine view out across the moors and hills. On the lawn was pitched a large white canvas tent. Very large, in fact. It looked like it was made of several pieces of canvas stitched together. Sitting in front of its opening was a man with the most flyaway hair I had ever seen, and a grey beard so long it was tucked into his waistband. His face was brown from too much sun, and he grinned at me toothily.

'You shouldn't be here!'

'Oh...um, sorry...' I stammered, although he had said it cheerfully enough, and he waved away my weak apology as soon as it began.

'Don't worry none,' he said, and patted the grass next to him, inviting me to sit.

I backed away. 'I should really get back to my friends. I wasn't supposed to wander.'

The man laughed. 'Deirdre told you that, I expect. Don't you worry about her. I'll protect you.' He winked at me and patted the ground again.

Hesitantly, I moved towards him. He was sitting in front of a small storm kettle, out of which a thin stream of steam was just emerging.

'Tea?' he asked.

'Oh, uh, alright.' I'd just noticed something rather odd. Odder than a man camping out on the lawn of a perfectly pleasant house. Around his wrist was tied a very long piece of twine. I followed it with my eyes until I found the other end, which was tied to the handle of the farmhouse's back door. He saw me looking and grinned. 'Don't mind that. Deirdre did it for me. Stops me wandering off and getting lost.'

'Do you, um… often get lost?' I asked.

'Oh, yes!' he said happily, pouring the steaming water into a teapot he had produced from somewhere. 'All the time. Forget my own name if it wasn't written down.'

'What is your name?'

'Hmm?'

'I said, what is your name?'

He looked nonplussed for a moment, then, to my surprise, he turned out the left hand side of his jacket to reveal a label sewn inside. He read it, then said, 'Archibald Forestrusel Ham.'

'Mrs Ham is your wife?' I admit I was a little surprised. This man seemed more wild man than the respectable farmer I had been expecting.

His leathery brow creased. 'Who?'

'Deirdre?' I tried.

'Oh yes! Fine woman, is Deirdre. Have you met her?'

'Well, yes,' I said. 'She told me not to wander, remember?'

'Wonder about what?' he asked, smiling at me pleasantly.

'No, I mean not to wander off.'

'Good solid advice that,' he said. 'You never know where you might end up if you wander off! Mind you, this seems like a nice place.' He appraised the farmhouse as if he'd never seen it before.

'Don't you live here?' I asked, thoroughly confused.

'Where?'

'*Here*.' I gestured to the house and the surroundings.

'Do I?' said Archibald, if that was indeed his name, and scratched at his beard in a thoughtful manner. This seemed to make him notice the string around his wrist. He plucked at it in obvious confusion, pulling it until it twanged tight against the door handle, then laughed and said, 'Oh yes! Yes, I do live here.'

'Well, forgive me for saying so, sir, but you

don't seem very sure.'

The man chuckled, handing me a cup of hot water I assumed was meant to be tea. He'd forgotten to add the leaves to the pot. 'Oh, I try not to worry about being sure of things. I'm afraid I don't have the wossaname for it…memory!'

'Did something happen to you?' I asked, already forming a suspicion that I knew just what it had been.

'Possibly,' he said, stroking his long beard. 'I forget. You'll have to ask Deirdre; she'll remember.'

'Sounds like you're lucky to have her.'

'Oh, yes!' he said. 'She's my…what's it called? Hard thing…cold…you get them in the ground?'

'Rock?'

'That's the monkey! She's my rock!'

'Well, thank you for the tea,' I said, delicately putting down my half-empty cup. I had poured some of the water away when he wasn't looking. 'But I should really get back to my friends before Deirdre…I mean, Mrs Ham notices I've gone.'

I got to my feet, and Mr Ham sprang up beside me. 'I'll come with you!'

I hesitated. 'Is that wise? I wouldn't want you to get lost.'

'No fear,' he said, waving the string still attached to his wrist.

'Well, alright,' I said. 'I can introduce you, if you like?'

'Splendid!' he enthused.

My new friend followed me back down the

side of the house. I was worried he'd run out of flex on his tethering system, but it seemed Mrs Ham had allowed quite a long length to the string. It took us twice as long to get back to the farmyard as it had for me to reach the field where Mr Ham's tent was pitched. This was because the man kept getting distracted by things along the way and wandering off. When he spotted a patch of daffodils, I had to physically grab the string and tug at it to regain his attention. Thankfully, he didn't actually forget who I was along the way. That might have been awkward.

When we finally made it back, we found the others waiting patiently, as instructed.

'Well, hello, and who do we have here?' asked Mr Gout, who had been standing with his hands clasped behind his back, bouncing on his heels and whistling. He was obviously feeling much better.

'This is Mr Ham, Mrs Ham's husband…I think,' I said.

'Delightful to meet you, old fellow!' Mr Gout enthused, taking the farmer by the hand. I saw him take in the string tied around the wrist, following it back across the yard with his eyes. One brow arched, but he said nothing.

Mr Ham, however, had eyes only for Klous.

'My word…a giant toad in a coat!'

'Watch it, pal!' Klous said, waving a clawed finger toward the farmer.

'This is Klous,' I hurried to explain. 'He's a

Kobold, actually.'

'Charmed, I'm sure!' He seemed fairly calm about it; nevertheless, I was glad that Custard was somewhere out of sight.

I introduced the others quickly, although I had little hope he would remember who any of us were.

'Mr Ham lives in a tent behind the farmhouse,' I explained, giving them all a significant look.

'Do you indeed?' said Mr Gout, stroking his chin and regarding the wild-looking man with renewed interest. 'I've done a fair bit of camping myself, as it happens. Lovely in the summer, of course, but a bit of a bugger in the colder months.'

'Deirdre looks after me,' Mr Ham said happily, his attention already drifting around the farmyard.

'Does she indeed? How very interesting. I think we need to have a long conversation, Deirdre and I. When she returns from whatever it is she is doing, of course.'

'Probably poisoning the tea,' grumbled Mrs Winchester.

However, we didn't need to wait long for Mrs Ham's reappearance. We heard her before we saw her.

'Archie! Archie, what are you doing? Get away from those people!'

We all turned to see the furious woman scurrying across the yard towards us, like an angry hen.

Mr Ham looked at her without recognition for a moment, but then something seemed to drop into place and he beamed at her. 'Deirdre, dear, come and meet my new friends! This lovely young lady is called Turpentine,' he said, cupping my elbow with his hand for a moment. 'This fine woman, I believe, is called Mrs Draftmeister, and this is her husband, Mr Sprout. Oh, and I think this is their son...or possibly their pet, Mr Mouse.'

I dared not look at the others' faces.

Mr Ham beamed around at us. 'Did I get that all right?'

I coughed and shuffled my feet. 'Um... certainly, more or less.'

He looked thrilled. His wife, far less so. As I had been the last to speak, she focused her ire on me.

'How dare you! I specifically told you not to wander. Just who do you think you are, rooting about in other people's lives?'

'I didn't mean–' I began, but Mr Gout cut me off.

'Enough!' The sternness in his voice made us all jump. 'We can bicker till the cows come home, my dear, but we have far more important things to discuss.'

The woman scowled at him. 'Oh, do we indeed? Like what?'

'Like curses. I am cursed, Mrs Ham. But I believe you already knew that, don't you?'

She shrugged, but said nothing.

Mr Gout continued. 'Yes, you already knew that because I think you were there when it happened. Or at least nearby. And you, Mr Ham,' he turned his attention to the bemused-looking farmer. 'You, I believe, were very close indeed.'

'And what makes you say that?' Mrs Ham snapped.

'Do you know what happens when you get too close to a powerful curse as it's being cast?' he asked her.

'Of course I bloody don't!'

'Oh, but I think you do, my good woman. I think you know *exactly* what happens.'

'*I* don't know what happens,' I pointed out.

Mr Gout smiled, but kept his eyes locked on Mrs Ham. 'You get caught up in the spell. It depends how close you get, of course, and the exact nature of the hex being cast. Sometimes you just get a bit of a funny turn. Most times, any effects will wear off after a few days; maybe a few weeks. With powerful curses, though, things can be different. But I'd be willing to bet you know a thing or two about that, wouldn't you, Mrs Ham? Mr Ham?'

Mr Ham looked confused. 'Are you suggesting Deirdre goes around casting powerful curses?'

'No, Archie,' said Mrs Ham. 'He's suggesting that you got caught up in a powerful curse.'

'*My* powerful curse,' said Mr Gout. 'Or rather,

I should say, the curse that was cast on me. I suspect you were close enough at the time, my good man, to get a considerable amount of blowback.'

The man still looked lost. 'Blowback?'

'Tell me if this rings any bells. Lost time? Lost memories? Trouble remembering events and people from your past life? Being unable to sleep under a proper roof?'

Then Mrs Ham exploded. 'I knew it! All these years I KNEW it was you who were to blame! Do you know what you did to my Archie? Do you have any idea of the damage you've caused?'

'Mr Gout ain't caused nothing!' Mrs Winchester warned. 'Didn't you listen? He didn't cast the curse, he received it!'

'Do you think I care about that? Do you think that mattered? Whoever cast the damn thing, it doesn't matter. What matters in that my husband has been unable to sleep in his own home ever since. What matters is that for years, he couldn't remember who I was...who *he* was. *What matters* is that even now, so many years later, if I don't tie my husband's wrist to the kitchen door, he will wander off and I might not see him again for weeks! Whether you cast the curse or not, you are the reason for it. *You are the man who ruined our lives!*'

PART SIX

As awkward dinner parties go, it was one of the worst of my life.

We sat at what turned out to be a very large dining room table, set in a room frankly too small for it. If I shifted too much in my chair, I hit my elbow on the whitewashed stone wall behind me.

I wasn't sure what I had expected to find in the interior of the Hams' family home, but it was clear that Mrs Ham maintained it with the same military ferociousness as Mrs Winchester did Oystercatcher Cottage. Everything was neat. Everything was clean. You would not have found a dusty shelf or a dirty glass in the entire place.

Yet there was one thing that Mrs Ham had not been able to scrub away, although I was willing to bet she had tried her hardest.

Throughout the house there pervaded a deep sense of emptiness.

It was as though the family had been away, and everything waited, clean, neat and organised, for their eventual return. It made me feel even more sorry for Mrs Ham than I had before. I couldn't help thinking of her, sitting alone in this house, night after night, while her husband slowly forgot who she was, just outside the door. It made me desperately sad.

Mrs Ham and Mrs Winchester were still refusing to speak to each other. Mr Gout had slipped into one of this thoughtful, some might say sullen, silences. Mr Ham, meanwhile, seemed to have temporarily nodded off. He leant far back in his chair with his head back, mouth open, and every few seconds let loose a muffled, grunting snore. Custard had retreated into Mrs Winchester's bag. I could just make out his ghostly glow from where it hung on the back of her chair.

That left me and Klous. Unsure what to say, given the circumstances, we sat mostly in silence, making eye contact every few seconds and giving each other a series of desperate grins, shrugs and other equally hopeless facial expressions.

Mrs Ham had provided a large pot of tea and finger sandwiches cut so neatly I felt she must have used a set square. She served Mrs Winchester first, with a bright, brittle smile that could have shattered into pieces so sharp they'd take someone's eye out. Mrs Winchester had received the fare with matching polite disdain. When their eyes met over the teapot, I felt sure the water inside would boil anew.

The rest of us were then served in stony silence. I managed a polite 'Thank you', which was ignored, and Klous produced a cheery 'Ta, Missus!' which was met with such a scandalised expression that he hadn't dared utter a word since.

And so we sat, sipping tea and nibbling ham sandwiches, each deep in our own private thoughts. I felt the afternoon might wear on forever.

Then Mr Gout shattered the fragile peace.

'So,' he said, looking up suddenly at Mr Ham, as though he were continuing a conversation that had merely paused for a moment, 'You caught my curse then, did you?'

I stifled a small gasp at the abruptness of the question and there was a little tinkle as a nervous Klous dropped his teacup.

'Sorry,' he murmured, dabbing at the spreading brown stain on the white tablecloth with a napkin. Mrs Ham, however, had not noticed. Her eyes were burning into my master with a hatred that was a little frightening. Mr Ham, startled fully awake, however, looked, as I was already finding he often did: bemused.

'Curse?'

'I imagine that is why you sleep in the garden and occasionally forget who you are, yes?' Mr Gout said simply.

'Forget who I am?' Mr Ham said, his voice sounding vague and his eyes drifting to his wife, who had crushed a finger sandwich in her fist without realising. But she said nothing.

Mr Gout continued anyway. 'It's fascinating, really. After all these years.... Tell me, did we know each other at all, before? Ha! A silly question, of course. How would we, either of us, remember?' He gave a low chuckle and Mr Ham grinned in return, though I suspected he was not really following the conversation.

'Of course you knew each other!' Mrs Ham snapped.

Mr Gout turned to her. 'We did? Interesting. And your husband's current affliction, that was a result of our association?'

The woman glowered. 'If by that you mean he was in the wrong place at the wrong time, then yes.'

'If you know that, then you know exactly when the curse occurred,' I blurted out with sudden realisation.

The woman turned her vicious eyes on me. 'Of course I know! Did you imagine my husband returned one night, a ruined man, and I somehow failed to notice?'

'Err, no...sorry,' I muttered.

The woman's eyes grew distant for a moment, and the harsh look on her face shifted to one of simple sadness. 'I remember that night as though it were yesterday...'

'Well, my good woman, there you have me at a distinct disadvantage,' said Mr Gout. 'For I neither remember it nor really know what it is that I cannot remember. Much is a blank to me. I sense from you that you feel I should feel some shame for what has happened to you and to your husband. You feel angry with me. Perhaps you have a right to be. I cannot say. It is hard for me to know how I should feel when I remember none of it.'

The anger returned to the woman's face. 'I don't want to hear your sob story!'

Mr Gout simply nodded. 'I've no doubt. I, however, must hear yours. If nothing else, perhaps it will make me feel the guilt you so obviously believe I should.'

The woman hesitated. An unreadable look passed across her face. She eyed my master speculatively. 'Just exactly how much *do* you remember...of your family? Of...'

'Of what happened to my brother?' Mr Gout finished for her, guessing her question.

'Well, yes. What happened to your brother... and what happened after that?'

Mr Gout sat back in his chair with a deep sigh. 'I admit,' he said slowly, as if forcing each word out against his better judgement, 'that there are one or two...let's call them vagaries, about some specific details. It has taken many years for the memories to return to me. But I believe I can now give a fairly decent account of what transpired.'

He stopped there and stared at the

tablecloth.

'And that was?' Mrs Ham insisted.

I opened my mouth to protest. Although I was vibrating with a fierce curiosity, it was clear that Mr Gout did not wish to go on. He spoke before I could say anything, however.

'Alright,' he said shortly, almost snappishly. 'If we must do this, then I suppose we must. I will tell the tale in exchange for yours. But I confess, Mrs Ham, I find it a hard bargain.' He looked at the old woman stonily. She glared back, unrepentant.

'However,' he continued. 'This is not a tale to be told over tea. It requires something stronger.'

'Now yer talking!' Klous said, grinning wickedly and rubbing his hands together in anticipation.

Mr Ham spared him a disgusted glance. 'Very well,' she conceded. 'I have a little brandy that I suppose will do.'

'Very well indeed,' Mr Gout agreed with a nod.

Silence reigned as the woman extricated herself from the table, disappeared into the adjoining kitchen, then returned with tray, bottle and glasses. Mr Gout did not speak until he was clutching a good measure of the amber liquid. He did not drink it straight away, however. Instead, he clasped it in both of his podgy hands, seeming to gain strength from it purely via osmosis. His eyes remained fixed on the glass as he talked.

'Matthias and I were about as different as

two brothers could be. He was dark where I was fair. He was wiry. Slender, quick of movement and quicker of thought. Some would say sly. There was always something a little feline about Matthias, even before...what happened. I, on the other hand...' He finished the sentence there, gesturing to the broad girth of his stomach with a twitch at the corner of his mouth. 'Well, I had other attributes. He was the elder by several years and, as a young boy, I idolised him. He was clever. Popular. He had a way with people that I simply lacked. The life of the party, so to speak, when I was more likely to be alone in the library with a book.

'He went to Oxford when I was still in short trousers, there being ten years between us.. I forget what it was he studied. I think he would have hardly remembered himself half the time. His heart was not in academic study. He was interested in other pursuits. I remember distinctly the look of frustration – no, exasperation – on my parents' faces the day he returned home, having been asked to leave. Sent down, as they call it. They soon forgave him, of course. Everyone always forgave Matthias. He spent the next few years dabbling in various vocations, though none so seriously that I feel it worth recording them for you here. By the time I left for prep school, before attending Oxford myself, he was in his late twenties and looked to be settling into the life of an upper-class loafer quite nicely. Which just goes to show that appearances can be deceiving.

'Unbeknownst to the rest of the family, Matthias's university days had left a far greater mark on his life than we could ever have guessed. I learnt the full story from him much later – at least, I think I did. It is a little hazy. Regardless, I can relate it to you now. My brother's proclivities while attending Oxford saw him fall in with a crowd of like-minded souls. They quickly slipped in to a pattern, a bubble of the feckless student if you will, rising late, in time for dinner, or perhaps lunch, then visiting the various clubs to which their privilege bought membership. They then ate, drank and caroused their way through to the lighting of dawn or the emptying of their pockets, whichever came first. A regular enough scene.

'It was in his second year of attendance that this pattern was broken. He, or possibly another member of his group, I forget, was approached by a man with information about a very select club. They had, so said the man, been selected for membership. Having somewhat tired of their regular haunts, Matthias and his friends were eager to explore this little mystery. Too eager, in all likelihood. They did not possess within their number a member to offer what they could have used most dearly; a cool head upon steady shoulders. Or rather, if they did, it was Matthias himself, and he was clearly of no mind to listen to the more restrained parts of his personality. If they had, if *he* had, then perhaps they might have questioned more this secretive club and their surprise invitations.

'For of course, the club did not turn out to be quite what any of them expected.'

Here Mr Gout paused to take a sip of brandy and Mrs Ham filled the silence, her eyes shrewd. 'It has a name, this secret club?'

My master gave a long sigh, then lifted his head. But it was to me his wandering eyes were drawn, and the expression on his round face was at once abashed and apologetic. I wondered at its meaning until he spoke again.

'It had several names, I believe. And I've no doubt that its true name was not revealed to Matthias and his friends at that time, but as they, and later I, would eventually learn, it was just one arm of a far older organisation. That organisation has become known as The Cult of the Green Lily.'

'*What*?' I blurted out before I could stop myself, and all eyes were drawn to me. 'The...the green lily...like the one we found on the Alp that attacked my grandmother? Like we found on the Zombie who wiped out Klous's crew? You...you *knew* about it all this time? You knew who was behind it all?'

Mr Gout looked uncomfortable. 'In a sense, yes,' he said.

My eyebrows dropped into a scowl. A fiery rage had ignited in my chest. 'In a sense? *In a sense*! What does that mean? You told me you couldn't remember where you'd seen the sigil before. Was that a lie?'

He clasped his hands together on the tabletop and looked at me straight. His blue eyes were as serious as I had ever seen them. 'That was no lie, Miss Trussel. I truly did not remember any of this. Not when we first met and found that sign of a lily in the Alp's hat. But that day, that moment in your grandmother's attic...it was as though something came loose in my mind. Like the glass walls of some small chamber in my brain cracked, and ever since, the memories have been leaking out.'

There was silence for a moment, then, 'How long?' I asked. 'How long since you remembered?'

'I became convinced in Thicklewood,' he said. 'The memories were clear enough to me by then.'

Weeks. He'd known for weeks and hadn't told me.

'I see,' I said, breaking eye contact. I sat back in my chair and folded my arms across my chest.

'My dear Clementine–' Mr Gout began, but stopped when Mrs Ham cleared her throat noisily. He sighed and wiped a hand across his face. 'We will discuss it later. For now, I must continue my story.'

I said nothing, and after a pause of several seconds, he resumed.

'This new club, as it was relayed to me many years later, started out innocently enough. Just another place to waste away the nights, and any privileges their stations in life provided them. But it seems that changed pretty soon. The members of this new club had interests other than those the usual gentleman's clubs provided. Supernatural interests. I believe it started on a fairly small scale. The odd seance, parlour trick, that sort of thing. No doubt it all felt very exciting and risqué for my brother and his friends. They were young. And foolish. For it seems clear now that they were being groomed.'

'*Groomed*? Groomed for what exactly?' I snapped the question at him, unable to keep the anger out of my voice.

'For service. Service to the Green Lily. My friends and I have seen one example of what that sort of service can look like.'

'We have?' said Klous.

'The Zombie,' I said. 'Are you saying your brother and his friends were…'

'No. No, they were spared that fate, at least. But there are plenty of other ways to compel someone into doing as you wish. I cannot say how it began, but by the time my brother left Oxford and returned home, I know he was held under the Green Lily's sway by the simplest method of them all. Blackmail.'

'I'm confused. What were they blackmailing him to do? What did they want?' asked Mrs Ham.

Mr Gout sighed. 'An organisation such as the Green Lily has its fingers in a lot of pies, most of them – if you'll excuse the pun – quite unsavoury. My brother and his friends were from good families. That means connections. That means access. I cannot tell you half of the things they had my brother do, for I simply do not know. However, I do know that he became quite an accomplished thief. I suspect, however, this was the thin end of the wedge.'

'What exactly do they want, the Green Lily?' I asked.

Mr Gout shrugged. 'Power. Influence. I am not so intimately familiar with them to say more than that. All I know is that their quest for it destroyed my family.'

He said this last hotly, then fell into silence. He stared through the brandy in his hands, clearly lost in the jumble of his own past.

Mrs Ham cleared her throat pointedly. Mrs Winchester shot her a filthy look, but the woman either didn't see it or pretended not to notice. I glanced at Mr Ham, who was gazing at the ceiling, a vacant smile on his haggard face. Soon after, my master spoke again.

'I cannot tell you the exact details of what happened, for I do not know them. I do not think I ever did. But while the rest of the family believed Matthias to be nothing more than an idle layabout, he was busy working for the Green Lily. If there were signs, my parents certainly did not pick up on them. By this time, I was away preparing for Oxford university myself, and saw little of them. Then one day I received a letter telling me my brother was dead.'

'How…how did it happen?' I asked. I felt bad about asking such a bald question, but I was still angry at him for keeping all this from me for so long.

'The letter did not say. Naturally, I hurried home at once. But by the time I arrived…well, things had deteriorated further.'

'This part I remember for myself,' said Mrs Ham.

Mr Gout looked vaguely surprised. 'Really?'

The woman gave a single curt nod. 'Oh, yes. Believe me, you don't forget a thing like that. I remember the grief your parents felt at the news of your brother's passing…and the horror at his return.'

'He came back as a revenant. A cat,' I said.

'Yes,' said Mr Gout. 'By the time I arrived home, the place was in an uproar. I remember my mother was completely hysterical.'

'So would you have been! The poor woman had lost a son only to have him return as some half-crazed beast,' said Mrs Ham. 'I was here, on the estate, when he first appeared. My mother was a maid for the family and woud often bring me along.'

'How did you know it was him?' I asked.

She looked thoughtful. 'It's hard to say. We didn't, not immediately. But it wasn't long before we realised. It just…*felt* like Matthias. That's the only way I can describe it. It was all quite a shock, of course. These things…these otherworldly things...we were none of us prepared. But when the cat appeared, there was somehow no questioning it. It was your mother who recognised him first. Once we realised we thought...well, we thought we might be able to reason with him. This was Matthias, after all. But...'

'But there is no reasoning with a revenant,' Mr Gout supplied.

'He attacked you?' Mrs Winchester asked.

'By the time I arrived home,' said Mr Gout. 'My parents were already dead.'

I let out an involuntary gasp. 'He *killed* them?'

My master nodded forlornly. 'As you know well enough yourself, Miss Trussel, a revenant left to its own devices only grows more powerful and violent with time. I arrived too late to help my parents. Not that I could have been of much help, not then. I still knew nothing of the supernatural. That was to change quickly, however.'

'Where were you by this time?' I asked Mrs Ham. 'How is it you were not also...'

'I asked myself that same question many times after that night,' the woman said. 'But the simple truth is, I do not know. All I know is that Matthias only seemed interested in his parents. Once they...once they were gone, he simply let us leave. We, that is my mother and I, went to the only place we could think of going. St Bartholomew's, the church in the village..'

'The church? Your mothers employers are

lying dead and you decide to go to Sunday service?' Mrs Winchester said, scathingly.

Mrs Ham coloured. 'We didn't know what we were dealing with! What should we have done? It was the only place we could think of that might hold some answers.'

'Did they?' I asked.

She scowled. 'No. They thought we were insane. Even suspected us of the deaths until the authorities ruled it to be an animal attack.'

The room fell into silence. I was struggling with conflicting emotions. On the one hand, I was still furious with Mr Gout for keeping so much from me. But then to think of all he had gone through; all that he had lost. It was hard to stay angry in the face of such tragedy.

'Well,' Mrs Ham said at last. 'I think I can pick up the story from here.'

Mr Gout's eyebrows rose. Mrs Ham noticed his surprise, even if he didn't speak.

'I don't know everything,' she said. 'And I'm sure I don't want to. But an event like that…well, it changes a person. I grew, married Archie, but I never forgot. And whether you were aware of it or not, we kept a close eye on you from then on, Theophilius, whenever we could..'

'I…I did not know that,' my master said.

'Well, you had other things on your mind. Can't blame you for that, I suppose. It wasn't simple, mind you – you never stayed in one place for long.'

Mr Gout nodded. 'I had a lot to learn.'

'So we gathered.'

'You...you were aware of my study of the supernatural?'

'We were. Even then, we suspected it would lead to no good. But...well, with what had happened to your family, we thought you needed it. Needed something to focus on. We hoped no harm would come of it. Perhaps if we had intervened, then...but we thought it best to let you get it out of your system.'

'You could not have stopped me,' Mr Gout said. He was looking into space, as if struggling to remember. 'In those early days, my curiosity was driven by the purest of all motivators. Anger. Revenge, maybe. I don't think I even knew. But there was so much to learn. This new world ran deep, far deeper than I'd expected when first I started digging. But from there, I'm afraid my memory is still foggy at best.'

'Well, mine is clear,' said Mrs Ham. 'As I say, we followed your exploits as best we could, but then we lost track of you. We heard nothing of your whereabouts for several years. We watched the house and waited, but it remained empty. Eventually, we accepted that the worst must have happened. But then came that night...the night that changed everything once again.

'As I said, we were always watching the house, hoping for a sign of you, even then. Well, on that night, thirty years ago, we got it. It started with strange lights in the sky. Over by the castle. Purple, blue and green illuminations, like that thing up North…the aurora borealis, like that. Well, we knew it had to be you. The place had lain quiet and still all those years. Although the uncanny hadn't been completely absent from our lives in all that time – as I'm sure you know, once one has one's eyes open to that world it is hard to shut them again – Mr Ham and I had experienced nothing on the scale of what happened to your family since. Now here were these unexplained lights, right over the very house they'd left behind. Who else could it be but you? We rushed over there right away.

'How I wish to god every day since that we had not.

'We knew something was badly wrong the moment we arrived. Nothing that looks like that in the sky can be good. We also knew it was supernatural. For the second time in our lives, we were getting a proper glimpse into that world. Our first one should have warned us to stay away. But we were still desperate for news about you.' She glared at Mr Gout here, as if the whole thing were his fault.

'What did you see? What happened next?' I asked.

'The colours in the sky, which had started as almost a dramatic sunset, swirled in a most unlikely manner, like water down a plughole. That was when we truly got scared. We'd have run then

– we almost did – but that's when you made your grand entrance, Mr Gout.'

'I did?' he said, looking startled. 'I have no memory of any of this.'

'Well, that doesn't surprise me, even without all this curse business. You seemed barely conscious. Which wasn't surprising either, given how you came flying out of the sky faster than one of them motor cars!'

'I came flying out of the sky?'

'You did. Just like a spider through a plughole! Popped into existence about twenty feet off the ground and landed with such a thud, I felt sure it must have broken some bones. That made us stay. Mr Ham here, well, he didn't hesitate, not once he saw you. He went running across the gravel to where you'd fallen and helped you to your feet. You were dazed, didn't know where you were. Or who we were. Just kept saying the same thing over and over…'

My master perked up at that. 'What was that?' he asked, his voice sharp.

'Beware the white lady.' It was Mr Ham who spoke, making me jump, as I had assumed he had long ago stopped paying any attention to the conversation. He said it in a dreamy voice, head still tilted towards the ceiling, eyes now closed.

Mrs Ham nodded. 'Buggered if I know what it meant.'

Mr Gout looked blank. 'What was I saying that for?'

'How in heaven should I know?' Mrs Ham snapped. 'To be honest, we were both more concerned with how you'd just appeared out of the sky. We didn't have long to think about it, though, because you were just the first to appear.'

Mr Gout positively leapt forward out of his seat this time. 'I was not alone? There were others with me?'

'Just one. One...lady.'

'Who was it?'

'Do you know, I didn't think to get her name,' the old woman retorted. 'What with all the cursing and whatnot! And she didn't fall like you. She just sort of stepped out of nowhere, like she was simply walking into another room. Then she...well, she floated down next to us on the ground.'

'What did she look like?' I asked.

Mrs Ham appeared to think about this for a long time. Eventually she said, 'It's the strangest thing...I remember her voice most. It was high and cold. She spoke like she felt nothing. Nothing at all. She was wearing a dress...a dress like nothing I ever saw before, nor since. The colours, the lace...it was like something out of a storybook. Something a queen might wear. She was slim...slight, I'd even say. She walked slowly, smoothly, like...oh it sounds silly...'

'Go on?' Mr Gout prodded gently.

'Well, to tell the truth, she walked like she wasn't really there.'

'What do you mean?'

'It's hard to describe. But I felt like if she had happened to walk into a wall, she'd have passed right through it like it was mist. She didn't of course; she was with all of us out in front of the house, on the gravel. But it's funny, I'd swear her feet didn't make a sound...on the gravel, I mean. Me and Mr Ham, and you, Mr Gout, we were crunching with every step. Not her, though. She glided over the ground like it wasn't there.'

'And her face?'

'Well, that's the thing...I can't remember. And when I say that, I want you to understand that I have thought about that night every day of my life since. Gone over it in my mind a hundred thousand times. But I can't picture her face. Not at all.'

'That seems strange,' I said.

'It's more than strange! Bloody unnatural, it was. I think she was hiding it somehow.'

'Like with a scarf?'

'No! I'd have remembered something like that. I mean with magic.'

'You believe she was a practitioner?' Mr Gout asked.

'Given she'd just appeared out of thin air and brought you with her, I'd say so, yes!'

'You believe it was her who opened the portal?'

'Portal?'

'That is, by your descriptions, what we appeared through.'

'Well then, yes. Like I say, you were insensible. Then there was what she did next.'

'Which was?'

'She looked around. Looked at everything like she'd never seen it before. The trees. The castle. Even the bleeding gravel. Except she didn't look at us once. Not once. Acted like we weren't even here. To be honest, by this point, I was thinking we *shouldn't* be there. This was none of our business. I tried to drag Mr Ham away, but...'

'She cast the curse, didn't she? This mystery woman,' I asked.

Mrs Ham nodded. 'I believe so. I'm no expert in these things, of course.'

'How did it happen?'

'I couldn't rightly say,' the old woman said. 'It wasn't like she whipped out a magic wand and waved it about or anything.'

'You said her voice was cold,' Mr Gout observed. 'So she must have said something?'

Mrs Ham pursed her lips. 'She seemed to be...gloating.'

'About what?'

She shrugged. 'Beating you, maybe? It wasn't clear. But she kept saying now you would truly know what it felt like. Now you would suffer like she had suffered. You would be truly alone.'

'I see,' my master said, looking thoughtful.

'And then she...did whatever she did. Next thing I knew, I was waking up on the ground, completely alone. She had gone, you had gone, even Mr Ham had gone. That was when I truly panicked. I ran around shouting for him till I was near collapse again. I eventually found him wandering in a nearby sheep field. He had no idea who I was. No idea who *he* was. Which was when I knew that whatever the strange woman had done to you had also been done to my husband. That our association with your cursed family had undone us, at last.'

Mr Gout looked deeply troubled. All he uttered were the same two words: 'I see.'

'*Do you*?' the woman snapped.

'What about the monster?' I chimed in quickly.

She turned her icy gaze to me. '*Monster*? You mean the plant, I suppose? It's been there ever since that day. To keep people out, I suppose.'

'It's a plant?' I said in surprise.

She glowered at me. 'Of course it's a plant – didn't you see all its vines?'

PART SEVEN

The Wild Garlic Inn, despite being located in a quiet rural area, was the sort of establishment that hires a maitre d' with the uncanny ability to look down his nose at you, even when you are significantly taller than him. This particular gentleman, being barely five feet tall, deployed this skill often, and with apparent enthusiasm. That is, until Mr Gout, towering over the man, enquired if he was feeling quite well, at which point the man stopped looking snooty just long enough to show us to our rooms. He did raise an eyebrow to dangerously high levels, however, when he learnt that Mr Gout would like to sleep in the stables.

My room was on the second floor, and was possibly the most luxurious accommodation I had ever spent the night in. Mr Gout must have been feeling generous. It made me feel all the more guilty that he was having to rough it once again. Perhaps, I thought to myself, the next day we would finally break the curse and he could spend the night under a proper roof. His *own* roof.

That, of course, would mean getting past the beast with a thousand tentacles.

Vines, I corrected myself. They were vines, not tentacles, although the distinction did not make me feel better about our chances. If not for Klous, we might all be slowly rotting plant fertiliser right now.

It had been impressive, the fireball. It reminded me that Klous was a powerful creature, even if he did look like a giant toad and spent most of his time bickering with Mrs Winchester. He had also opted to stay in the stables, although of course the Inn's staff were not aware of this. There was only so much they could be expected to put up with, I supposed.

'It's no captain's quarters,' the little Kobold had said, 'But horses often make better company than you humans.'

Mrs Winchester was in the room next to mine. I could hear her pacing. It did not particularly surprise me that she was still up. The last few hours had certainly left us all with a lot to think about. The little tea party with the Hams had broken up not long after I'd brought up the monster. It was clear an invitation to stay would not be forthcoming, so we had driven, mostly in silence, to The Wild Garlic.

I was also finding it hard to sleep, despite being exhausted from the day's events. I suppose almost being eaten by the bedding plants will do that to a person.

I was also worried about the next day.

Just how would we deal with the thing in the corridor of Castle Gout? Magical gardening shears? Somehow I doubted it.

But more than that, I no longer knew if I trusted Mr Gout. He had hidden far too much from me and I was still angry. Angry and suspicious of what else he might be hiding.

I sighed and rolled over, beating my pillow into a more comfortable shape.

I just had to trust that my master had a plan. One that wouldn't get us all killed.

As I lay awake, my thoughts returned to the strange, real-looking boy I had seen in the grounds of Castle Gout. I could picture the shape of his jawline, and the green of his eyes, almost like fresh spring shoots...

Sleep was a long time coming.

#

I was soon to discover that Mr Gout did indeed have a plan. It just didn't involve the rest of us.

I awoke sometime before dawn, slowly coming to and staring at the ceiling veiled in deep shadows. I was wondering what had awoken me when I felt a movement at the foot of the bed. I stiffened, a jolt of primal fear running through me. I was just trying to decide whether to scream when a familiar voice said '*Pssst!*'

'Um…Klous?' I whispered.

''Course it's me! Who'd you think it was?' the little creature muttered, crawling up the bed towards me. I repressed a shudder. No one should have deal with this sort of thing before breakfast.

'What are you doing in my bedroom?' I asked, trying to keep my voice casual.

'We've got a big problem,' he said. 'He's gone.'

'Who's gone?'

'Theophilius! Who'd'ya think?'

I sat bolt upright, a nasty feeling swilling in my stomach. 'What do you mean by *gone*, exactly?'

'I mean gone. Scarpered. Disappeared. Sneaked off and left us in the lurch!'

I swore and shot out of bed. 'He's gone to the castle, hasn't he?'

'Of course he has! What are we gonna do?'

I pointed to the door. 'Well, you're going to wait outside while I get dressed. Better yet, wake up Mrs Winchester.'

The Kobold made a face. 'Do I have to? You know what she's like!'

I assured him he did, and he gracelessly left the room, grumbling all the way. I dressed quickly, splashed some water in my face, and was outside in the hall in less than five minutes. Klous was standing outside Mrs Winchester's door, looking sour.

'Gave me a right talking to, she did,' he complained.

'Well, if you woke her the same way you woke me, I'm not surprised! Where is she?'

'*Preparing herself,*' Klous quoted, in a passable impression of the woman's Welsh accent.

'I can't wait,' I said. 'I'm going after Mr Gout. You two follow when you can. We have to stop him from doing something stupid!'

'Might as well try to stop the grass from growing,' I heard Klous mutter, as I hurried down the hotel hallway with a growing feeling of doom.

PART EIGHT

I looked up at the huge black outline of Castle Gout. It was silhouetted in the grey morning light and looked more diabolical than ever. I was sure, if I squinted hard enough, I could see the shapes of vines twisting and writhing all over the walls. It looked like one gargantuan monster, and I quailed at the thought that Mr Gout might have gone inside.

I quailed all the more at the thought that I might have to follow him.

What had he been thinking, running off like that? It wasn't like him. At least, I tried telling myself that. But I knew the truth. The truth was, this was exactly like him. I knew with almost certain clarity what he had been thinking. This was *his* problem. *His* battle. No reason to get the rest of us killed. Better to go alone. He probably even thought he was being noble. But you can be noble and stupid at the same time. The two are not mutually exclusive. The noble part I had no problem with that was just like Mr Gout. But the stupid part? That's what bothered me. Mr Gout was many things, but stupid was most certainly not one of them. He must have known that the risks of re-entering the castle were too great. What had made him do it?

Something must have. It was the only explanation. Something had compelled him to this reckless course of action. I wished I knew what it had been.

I stood and waited in the soft dawn rain. My face ran with it, hair still unbrushed, gradually soaking through. I was thinking furiously yet getting nowhere. I couldn't follow my master inside, no matter how much I might have wanted to. I knew my limitations. It would serve neither of us if I got myself eaten by the thing that lurked inside, and I was under no illusions that was what would happen. We had barely escaped with our lives after our first encounter with the plant, and that had been mostly down to Klous and to luck. I'd been basically helpless.

I had to find another way to help. But how?

I was still wrestling with this thought when a movement caught my eye. A figure was trotting across the gravel between my hiding place, amid the undergrowth and the towering presence of the castle. For a moment, my heart leapt with joy and I thought I had been mistaken. After all, Mr Gout had not gone inside. But with a sinking feeling, I quickly realised the figure was far too small to be that of my master. I wiped the rain out of my eyes and squinted into the darkness. It was the boy! The one I'd met on the path when we'd first approached Castle Gout. The one who had warned us away.

Perhaps we should have listened.

But who was he? And what was he doing running around the grounds of a dangerous abandoned mansion in the rain at dawn? I felt even more sure that my initial instincts about the boy had been right. He knew something. He was involved. I had no idea how, but he was.

I decided to follow him.

Creeping from my hiding place, I moved swiftly but silently after the retreating figure. I didn't think the boy himself would be dangerous. After all, he hadn't attacked us the first time we'd met. But I didn't want him to know I was here. Not yet. I wanted to see what he was up to first.

I followed the fleeting figure in a sort of half-crouched run, attempting to balance the need to keep up with his surprisingly fast progress and not be heard or seen. It is quite possible that stealth is not my strong suit. But luckily for me, the boy seemed to pay little attention to the undergrowth, and anything that might move clumsily along it. The black form of the mansion took up his entire attention. He kept glancing up at it as he ran. I felt I could almost hear him muttering to himself, but I dared not get close enough to find out what. He quickly covered the exposed ground in front of the castle, his feet crunching on the gravel, and moved away down the side of the building. I had to keep to the edges of the gravel expanse for fear of my footsteps being heard. But I just about kept sight of him as he hurried through a stone archway into what I could only assume were further grounds behind the house. I paused momentarily, trying to decide if entering the castle's grounds would be any safer than the mansion itself. But I figured the boy wouldn't enter if he thought it too dangerous. Of course, it was possible he was somehow involved with the creature inside the house, but it seemed unlikely. Mr Gout had said its creation must have taken powerful magic, and whatever the boy might be, I doubted he was an evil sorcerer.

I followed him through the arch, stepping around the rotten remains of a wooden door, and coming out into what appeared to be some sort of garden. Or the remains of one, at least. I felt there had probably been a lawn once, sweeping away from the walls of the castle, but now there was a sea of waist-high grass. It waved in the light breeze. Beyond it I could see the pointed tops of some sort of large glasshouse. The panes of glass had long since shattered and disappeared, leaving just the bones of the building, glinting palely in the weak dawn light.

The boy, however, was moving in the opposite direction, down what might have once been a cobbled pathway, although it was practically impossible to tell beneath the years of moss and leaf litter. It led past a jumble of bricks and wood I thought might have once been a barn, or even some stables, and on, through a second archway, into what I suspected must have been a walled garden. This arch was still complete with a door, which gave a squeal of tortured metal as the boy slipped through. I moved silently up to the door and stopped. I couldn't see what I might be walking into and, as the boy had just proved, it would be impossible for me to pass through the door quietly.

I was still fretting over what to do next when I heard the boy speaking from the other side of the door.

'Obsidian!' he called softly.

I frowned to myself. *Obsidian*?

'Obsidian!' the boy called again, a little louder.

My mind raced. Was he calling some sort of...demon? Was the boy more involved with the dark magic at play here than I had thought?

Then I heard the distinct meowing of a cat and I had to bite the back of my hand to stop myself from laughing. What an idiot I was. Obsidian was the black cat!

'There you are,' I heard the boy say from the other side of the door. 'I was worried something might have happened to you.' Then the boy chuckled, a surprisingly warm sound. 'Alright, alright, here!' he said, and I heard the unmistakable sound of the cat eating.

So the stray boy was feeding the stray cat.

Why, I wondered? What made either of them hang around this place?

'You need to be careful, Obsidian,' the boy said. 'Those strangers have riled up the monster no end. You shouldn't go into the mansion; it's not safe.'

I decided it was time to make my appearance. I pushed open the squeaky door and stepped through it in time to see the boy, stood on the remains of another cobbled path, frozen in shock. His feline friend was much quicker to react, and I heard a small hiss and saw the flash of a black tail disappear into a mass of brambles that must have once been a flowerbed.

The boy scowled at me, but he didn't run. 'What are you doing here?' he asked.

'I could ask you the same question.'

'You scared off Obsidian!'

'That's a funny name for a cat. Did you make it up?'

He glared at me. 'That's a funny face for a girl. Did you make it up?'

That stung more than I liked to admit. 'There's no need to be rude,' I said, a little petulantly. 'Besides, that didn't quite make sense, did it?'

'Rude?' he said. 'You mean like sneaking around in the dark, following people?'

'Well, I wouldn't have needed to follow you if you had just hung around long enough to explain yourself yesterday,' I said.

He scowled all the deeper. 'I thought I was pretty clear. Not that you listened.'

'Why would I listen to some wild boy who appears out of the undergrowth?' I asked. 'Who are you?'

'Grub,' he said.

'What?'

'You asked who I was!'

'You're claiming your name is Grub?'

'I'm not claiming anything. That's my name!'

'Your parents took one look at you and thought the perfect name would be Grub?'

'Shut up!' he growled. 'I suppose you think your name's better?'

'I'm Clementine.'

'What, like an orange?'

'No, like a clementine. Look, what are you doing hanging around this place, Grub?'

The boy looked at me coolly, perhaps deciding on his response. 'I live here,' he said. 'It's my castle.'

I raised an eyebrow. 'Is your surname Gout?'

'What? No. Why?'

'Then you're lying. This is Castle Gout, and it belongs to my master.'

Grub looked furious for a moment, but then his face relaxed into a speculative expression. 'He the fat man who went inside?'

'He's not fat!' I said defensively, although I knew it wasn't true, and this time it was

Grub's turn to raise an eyebrow. 'Look, whatever,' I continued. 'I don't have time for this. I need to know everything you know.'

'Oh yes? Everything I know?'

'Yes!'

'Alright.' The boy looked around, and his eyes rested on a patch of brambles. He pointed. 'Those are brambles,' he said, then pointed at his own foot. 'This is a foot.'

'What are you doing?'

He smirked. 'Telling you everything I know. It might take a while.'

'That's not what I meant and you know it!'

Grub folded his arms, still smirking. 'Oh, so what is it you meant, then?'

'Oh, I don't know,' I said. 'Maybe something about the giant killer plant that's taken over the mansion you say is your home?'

He lost his smirk. 'You shouldn't mess around with that thing. It's dangerous.'

I rolled my eyes. 'You don't say? Any more pearls of wisdom to share?'

He regarded me. 'Is this place really your master's home?'

'Yes,' I said.

'Then where's he been all these years?' he asked.

I hesitated. 'That's...complicated. How long have you been here?'

Grub shrugged. 'About a year.'

'Why?'

'What?'

'I mean, why are you here? It's not exactly the nicest or the safest place to be. Squatting?'

He frowned at that, but all he said was, 'It has its advantages. So why has your master let his own house fall into ruin?'

'I told you, it's–'

'Complicated, yeah. Look, girl, if you want my help, you'll have to do better than that.'

I bridled. 'It's Clementine. Don't call me girl!'

He just shrugged, and I sighed. 'Fine.'

I paused, trying to think of the best way to explain the situation while giving away the least amount of information. 'Look, Mr Gout has been kept away. But now he's back and we need to get into the castle to…find something. Something that will make the monster go away.'

'The monster's not hurting anyone,' Grub said. 'Not anyone who isn't stupid enough to go inside, and nobody around here comes anywhere near the place.'

'Have you met the Hams?' I asked.

The boy shrugged. 'I've seen them about, sure.'

'Well, the thing we're looking for will help them too.'

He contemplated me. 'You mean Mr Ham, don't you? You're saying you can undo whatever happened to him?'

'We hope so, yes,' I said.

'Alright. So what is this thing you're looking

for?'

I hesitated. 'That's a little harder to explain.'

'It's magic, isn't it?' he asked.

I looked at him sharply. 'What makes you say that?'

'Look, I'm not stupid, alright?' he said. 'I know that bloody great plant isn't natural. And I saw those creatures you came here with; the big frog and the see-through rabbit.'

I sighed. 'That's Klous and Custard,' I said. 'Klous is a Kobold…well, a Klabautermann, actually, which is a sea-faring type of Kobold, and Custard is, well, a rabbit. Only he's dead.'

Grub stared at me.

'Really?' he said.

I nodded. 'Truly.'

'You called your rabbit Custard, and you had the nerve to laugh at my name?'

'That's the bit that shocks you?'

'Bloody stupid name for a rabbit!' he grumbled. 'Should be called Flopsy or Buttercup or Burdock.'

'And boys should be called Peter or Michael or John!' I retorted. 'Anyway, I didn't name him. He's Mr Gout's rabbit.'

'You people are weird,' he said, but he was smiling.

'Says you, who lives in a haunted mansion and has a cat called Obsidian,' I pointed out.

'Obsidian's not mine either,' he said. 'I just like to keep an eye on him. Don't think he's got a family.'

'So really?' I asked. 'Why *are* you here?'

Grub looked like he wouldn't answer, but then he relented. 'No great mystery, really. Ain't got nowhere else to go, have I?'

'You're...homeless?'

The boy shrugged. 'I was making my way across the country from village to village, just trying to get by. Found this place. Found Obsidian. No one bothers us here. The locals steer clear and there are plenty of places to keep warm and dry without actually going inside the castle. The thing – the monster or whatever – it doesn't seem to mind unless you go inside.'

'It didn't, I don't know, disturb you at all that there was a man-eating plant in the house?' I asked.

'Gave me a bit of a shock to start with, sure. But like I said, I keep out of its way and it keeps out of mine.'

There was a moment's silence while I thought about all of this. I wanted to ask about Grub's parents. Where were they? What had made him end up here? I looked at him critically. For all his show of bravado, it was clear he was having a tough time. Not enough to eat. Nowhere to wash properly. And whatever he said, I doubt there was anywhere in the mansion's broken-down outbuildings that were truly warm and dry, especially through the winter. I wondered where he got his food from.

In the end, I didn't get to ask any of these questions. Grub, no doubt sensing where my questioning was going to lead, spoke up instead.

'Come on then,' he said, turning.

'Where are we going?' I asked.

'You want to know more about the monster? I've got something to show you.'

I looked up at the silhouetted mansion in the growing dawn light. Mr Gout was in there, suffering who knew what, even as I stood there, wracked with indecision. Deciding there was little other choice, I followed the boy.

He led me through the abandoned garden, toward the remains of the glasshouse I'd seen earlier. The garden was spooky in the pale light. Weeds choked what must have once been a regimented bed system so tightly it was hard to picture what the place must have been like in its heyday. The gnarled shapes of espalier apple trees rose to meet us as we passed, long since escaping their strict pruning and reaching for the sky with limbs that looked twisted and withered. After a while, Obsidian reappeared, emerging from the undergrowth and following us, winding in and out of Grub's legs as he walked. Grub made little noises, bending briefly to rub the cat's head. Obviously comforted, it purred, a deep rumble that I could hear clearly from my position a few steps behind.

The drizzle, though light, had not let up, and I was now uncomfortably damp. I wasn't about to mention this to Grub, though. I felt certain he had put up with far worse.

We arrived at the glasshouse, and my guide stopped outside.

'You ready for this?' he asked, looking at me over his shoulder and smirking slightly.

'It would help if I knew what *this* was.'

His smirk faltered, and he shook his head with a dry chuckle. 'What was I thinking? Of course you're ready. I expect you see this sort of thing every day.'

'*What* sort of thing?' He really was very irritating.

He pointed to where a thin path had been made through the weeds and brambles up to the dilapidated door of the glasshouse. 'Go look.'

I eyed him suspiciously, but decided it was unlikely this was some sort of trap. I moved past him up the path, slowing as I approached the door and peered inside.

I could see nothing in the chaos.

Just like the beds outside, the glasshouse was a riot of weeds and what had to be decades of unchecked growth. I tiptoed inside, flinching slightly as a piece of glass cracked under my foot.

'Careful,' Grub said. 'There's glass all over. I think the whole place was just left to fall apart.'

I nodded without turning around and continued my cautious exploration.

'What am I looking for, exactly?'

'Over to the right.'

I looked where I was bid, but failed to see anything that looked any different to the mass of green undergrowth and smashed terracotta pots and glass that filled the rest of the space.

Then my eyes caught a flash of movement.

My mouth dropped open.

'Is that…' I began, trailing off.

'You tell me,' Grub said. 'You're the witch.'

'I'm not a witch!' I snapped, not taking my eyes off…

How to describe what I saw?

The movement had come from the top of what remained of a rotten potting bench or table. It was strewn with the same mix of broken glass and terracotta as the rest of the place. But amid all of that was a single complete pot. Or almost complete. It had a sizeable chunk missing from one side and soil spilled out in a heap. But it was the pot's contents that had caught my eye. A single plant, little bigger than an average bedding plant, with small, spear-shaped leaves, and a solitary trumpet-shaped magenta flower.

It was waving thin little vines, as if reaching out to try and grab us.

'What on earth is that?' I said.

'Well,' said Grub, coming to stand next to me. 'It looks to me very much like a petunia.'

'What?' he added defensively, obviously reading my thoughts in my face.

'Nothing. Sorry…it's just, I didn't expect you to know what…well–'

'What a petunia looks like? I'm not an idiot.'

'No, of course. Sorry,' I said, flustered.

I bent closer to the animated little plant. 'Of course, petunias don't normally do *that*,' I pointed out as the vines whipped out towards me, stretching and waving in the air, eagerly.

'Remind you of anything?' Grub asked with a grin.

I regarded him stonily. 'If you're trying to tell me that huge thing in the castle is also a petunia, I–'

'It makes perfect sense!' he said.

'Oh yes, *perfect* sense.'

'Don't you see?' He pushed past me and rooted around beneath the potting bench. He lifted the remains of a broken pot for me to see. Inside were the desiccated remains of another petunia-like plant. I could just make out the same weird little tendrils as the one on the bench, which was now giving a spirited attempt at pulling itself across the rotten wood towards where Grub's head was hovering. He saw it and dropped the pot, backing away.

'I've found several of these,' he said. 'I think they're experiments.'

'What, like trial runs?' I asked.

He shrugged. 'Sure, why not?'

I considered. 'I guess it's possible someone was breeding the things.'

'Question is, what for? Doesn't your Mr Gout know anything about it? You said this was his house, didn't you?'

'That's…complicated,' I said, making my way back out of the ruined glasshouse. It was giving me the heebie-jeebies.

Grub followed. 'And here I thought we were friends,' he said.

I bridled. 'And what made you think that?' There was something about this boy that made me irritable.

Grub simply laughed at me, which did nothing to improve my mood. 'Look,' he said. 'If you want my help, then you're going to have to trust me.'

'Who said I–'

'Wanted my help? You were creeping around in the dark outside instead of going in to the house after your friend. You clearly need help.'

'Alright, fine,' I conceded. 'I need help. But how would you be able to give it?'

The boy leant nonchalantly against the rotten timbers of the glasshouse door. 'Obsidian and I may have a trick or two up our sleeves when it comes to the monster.'

'You know how to get past it?' I said excitedly.

Grub grinned. 'Maybe. If you tell me what's going on.'

I swallowed down my irritation and thought hard. Could I trust this boy? And even if I could, were these my secrets to tell?

I shot a glance up at the forbidding castle,

now just lit by the first rays of the morning sun. They did little to improve its menacing demeanour. Mr Gout needed help. I made my decision.

'Very well. What do you want to know?'

Grub took an excited step towards me. 'What is he, exactly, this Mr Gout of yours?'

'A human,' I said. 'Next question?'

Grub made a face, and I relented. 'Alright; he's a Paranormal Investigator. He investigates strange phenomena, like…'

'Like giant man-eating plants in castles?' Grub said.

'Right. Among other things.'

'So that would make you?'

'His apprentice.'

Grub actually looked impressed, but he quickly smothered the expression. 'Can you do magic?'

I hesitated, but answered. 'He can. I can't.'

The boy gave a low whistle. 'What sort of thing?'

I thought about it. 'Truthfully, I'm not always sure. But I've seen him calm an angry spirit and send it on to the next realm, if that's the sort of thing you mean.'

This time there was no disguising the look of surprise on his face. He took another step toward me. 'No way, really?'

'Really. And he knows about everything supernatural. He's very experienced.'

Grub was silent for a moment. He looked like he was searching for his next question, trying to decide what he wanted to know most. 'And how about you?' he said, coming closer again, until he was just a step in front of me. 'Have you calmed any angry spirits?'

'I...I've helped,' I stammered, suddenly very aware of how close he was. I could smell the dampness of his clothes and...something else. Something almost spicy. 'I fought off a Zombie once,' I said, trying to look nonchalant.

He gaped at me. 'You're kidding me? A Zombie? Those are real?'

I nodded.

'That's so creepy!' he said, although he looked thrilled about it. 'What happened?'

'We don't have time to go into all that right now,' I said.

He rolled his eyes. 'Come on. Just give me the short version.'

I was saved from answering by a sudden rustling in the undergrowth beside us. We both whipped our heads around in time to see Klous's bulbous eyes appear in the greenery. Grub yelped and jumped backwards.

Klous was grinning.

'I do hope I haven't interrupted anything?' he said, waggling an eyebrow at me.

To my horror, I began to blush.

Grub recovered himself quickly. 'You're Klous? The Klabautermann?'

Klous turned to look at him. 'And you are?'

'Th...this is Grub,' I said, cursing my flaming cheeks.

'Of course it is,' Klous said. 'Well, I hate to break up whatever little–'

'Grub says he can help us get past the monster!' I blurted out.

The little Kobold extracted himself from the weeds and regarded Grub with a disbelieving look. 'Oh yeah? Bit of a monster hunter, are we?'

Grub scowled. 'What? No. I just...well, I've had some experience with it, that's all.'

Klous shrugged. 'Well, whatever. The old witch sent me to find you.' He turned to me. 'If you're not too busy to help, after all?'

'Of course not!'

'You know a witch too?' Grub asked me.

'He means Mrs Winchester. She's not really a...she's a housekeeper.'

Klous grinned. 'There are many words to describe that woman. Housekeeper is just one of them.'

'Be nice!' I scolded him, but he simply shrugged and beckoned us to follow.

We did so, slipping through the soaking bushes until we came back out in front of the house. I shivered, wetter than ever. 'There are paths we could have taken, you know.'

Klous didn't respond. He hopped up the steps to the large front door, which was still hanging slightly ajar. As he approached, Mrs

Winchester's head poked out. She was scowling.

'Where have you been?' she demanded, then she caught sight of Grub and her lips went thin. 'Who's this?'

'I found them canoodling in the garden,' said Klous.

'*We were not canoodling*!' I practically shrieked, hurrying up the stairs and very pointedly avoiding making eye contact with Grub. My face felt so hot I was sure I must have been shining out like a beacon in the grey dawn light. I quickly explained to Mrs Winchester what Grub had told me.

'Well, I suppose we need all the help we can get,' she said, looking Grub up and down with pursed lips. 'Theophilius, the blasted fool, is somewhere in there, but I can't find any sign of him.'

'What about the plant?' I asked.

She shook her head. 'Gone. Or at least moved. The door it came out of last time is open, but it's not there.'

'Does it usually move?' I asked Grub, refusing to meet his eyes and looking very hard at his right earlobe instead. He nodded enthusiastically, apparently eager to be useful.

'It does,' he said. 'It can pretty much go where it likes inside the castle, so far as I've been able to tell. I don't go in much, but sometimes I see it through the windows.'

'How does it get about, exactly?' Klous

asked. 'It hasn't got legs, has it?' The Klabautermann shuddered, clearly appalled at the thought.

'Not that I've seen,' Grub admitted. 'Then again, I've never seen the whole thing at once. Just...parts. Tentacles, mostly.'

'Vines,' I corrected without thinking.

'What? Oh, right. Yes, vines. Anyway, they reach all over. I guess it's possible the thing never actually moves at all.'

'My boy, are you suggesting the thing is large enough that it can reach all parts of this castle without moving?' Mrs Winchester said, her face paling slightly.

Grub shrugged. 'Maybe. Dunno for sure.'

Klous shuddered again. 'Those are some long vines.'

'If that's true, then Mr Gout...' I trailed off.

'Mr Gout is far too full of himself to get killed by a giant petunia,' Mrs Winchester said firmly. 'Nevertheless, we had better find the idiot soon, or who knows what trouble he might have gotten himself into.'

There was a pause as we each peered into the darkened entrance hall. I cannot say for sure what the others were thinking, but I myself was seriously wondering what help we might be, even if we did find him. Klous had that fireball thing of his, but Mrs Winchester and I? She had Custard peeking out of her bag, but I doubted a giant plant would fear a dead rabbit.

'Now might be an excellent time for a trick or two, young man,' Mrs Winchester said to Grub.

He stood up straighter. 'Right. Follow me!' He made to step into the room, but Mrs Winchester put out an arm to check his stride.

'To where exactly?'

'There's a secret passage,' he explained. 'If we're quick, then we can get in before the plant finds us and it won't be able to follow.'

'A secret passage? Really?' I asked. 'This place has everything.'

'Oh yeah. Secret passages, broken greenhouses, terrifying monsters,' Klous muttered.

'Stop your complaining,' snapped Mrs Winchester, clearly impatient to be moving on. Klous stuck his large black tongue out at her back.

We followed Grub into the shadowy entrance hall, stepping lightly, none of us wanting to attract the plant's attention. Obsidian, having followed us thus far, hovered in the doorway, then trotted away on errands of his own. Custard jumped down from Mrs Winchester's bag and followed him. I made to chase after them, but the housekeeper shook her head. 'Priorities, Miss Trussel. Custard will be fine.'

Grub led us to the opposite side of the room from the door through which the creature had emerged the last time we were there. He ran his hand along a patch of dado rail, more or less exactly opposite where the other door had been, then pushed. There was a soft click, and a crack appeared in the wall that had been unnoticeable before. He turned back to us and grinned. Mrs Winchester made a shooing notion, ushering him forward. He pushed open the newly appeared door and disappeared into a black hole in the wall. We followed tentatively, Klous bringing up the rear and giving one last nervous look over his shoulder into the silent entrance hall, before Grub pushed the door closed with another click.

It was dark.

Very dark.

I willed myself to stay calm. It was just the lack of light. Nothing inherently dangerous about that. *Apart from what might be lurking in it*, my deeper thoughts added. I reached out with my hands to find the wall, then stifled a scream when they met Klous's cold, smooth, slightly damp skin.

'Well, what's the plan now, boy genius?' the little creature hissed. 'As lovely as it is to stand here with you all in complete darkness, we're supposed to be rescuing someone.'

'We just have to wait for a moment to let our eyes adjust,' Grub whispered back.

We stood in silence. There was something oppressive about the space. The air smelt dusty and stale, and I felt myself begin to sweat despite my wet clothes and the chill. I stared into the black until my eyes watered, trying in vain to hurry the process along. The house creaked unsettlingly. The only other sound was the breathing of my companions. I could pick out Klous's deep rasps from somewhere near my knees. Mrs Winchester's came strong and steady. Grub's breath was surprisingly light. In fact, unless I'd been specifically searching for it, I might have missed it all together.

Eventually, my eyes began to adjust. I made out a narrow corridor of sorts ahead of us. It didn't seem like easy going. Various bars of what I assumed was wood jutted out into the space at what appeared to be random intervals, although I'm sure they had a purpose.

'Follow me,' Grub said eventually, and we began walking again, or rather creeping. I felt more of an intruder than ever. It was as though we had snuck beneath the skin of Castle Gout, and now we were crawling through its skeleton. There was a thud and a muffled curse behind me. I guessed Mrs Winchester had misjudged one of the joists of wood.

'Where does this lead?' I whispered to Grub.

He turned back to look at me. 'It comes out at the top of the stairs to the lower level. I think it was originally meant to be used by servants so they could move about the house unobtrusively.'

'What's on the lower level?'

I could just make out the boy shrug. 'No idea,' he said. 'But from what I can tell, that's where the monster spends most of its time.'

Klous's hiss emanated from below us. 'And what exactly are we planning to do once we find it? We didn't fare too well in a head-on assault last time.'

Mrs Winchester sniffed. 'It took us by surprise. But you're right. We'll need a plan before we face the thing again.'

'I've got one,' said Grub. He sounded excited. 'At least I think so...'

'Well, enlighten us, why don't you?' Klous said.

'The last time I scouted this far into the house, I found a room close to the steps we're heading to, which was locked up tight. I picked the lock, and once inside, I found a whole load of bottles. All full of a grungy-looking green liquid.'

'What was it?' I asked.

I saw a flash of white teeth as he grinned at me. 'General Frobisher's Cavalry Strength Weed Killer. Effective On One Hundred Per Cent Of Even The Toughest Unwanted Plants. It was on the labels,' he explained after a moment of stunned silence.

'That's your brilliant plan? *Weed killer*?' I gaped at him in the darkness.

'We're dealing with a magically created menace here, boy,' Mrs Winchester added. 'Not a stubborn patch of dandelions!'

'Dandelions, petunias, it's all the same,' Grub protested. 'Seemed like a good idea to me. Anyway, there were bottles and bottles of the stuff. I figured it has to be there for a reason. Maybe whoever created the monster used it to protect themselves.'

'I suppose anything is possible,' Mrs Winchester admitted wearily. 'Well, it's the best plan we've got. Lead us to the weed killer, young man.'

#

It wasn't long before we reached the end of the passageway. Motioning for us to wait, Grub placed both of his hands against the wall and very gently pushed until there was a small click. A section of the wall swung outwards, emitting a brief but loud groan of hidden metal. I winced and saw Grub's shoulders tense. We all waited for several minutes, hardly daring to breathe, but eventually it seemed we were still alone. Grub beckoned us forward and the four of us slipped from the passage into another slightly larger, whitewashed corridor; clearly a part of the network of service paths all such great houses possessed. Through silent communication, we elected to leave the door to the secret passage open, deciding as one that it was better to risk it being found by the plant than have it make more noise as it closed. Grub beckoned us on and we followed. This new space struck chilly and damp, but it was a relief after the confines of the secret passage. It wasn't long before we found the stairs that Grub had promised. It was still dark in the servants' corridor, but the stone steps descended into an even blacker gloom below. I was secretly thankful that we were not headed that way. Grub led us quickly past the opening and I followed gratefully.

Nearly fifty steps on, we came to an unpainted door on the left.

'This is the one,' Grub whispered.

'Well, go on then, boy, don't let's stand about here all day!' Mrs Winchester's voice was low but brisk. I could tell she was anxious about Mr Gout. So was I.

Grub took her at her word and pushed open the door. I was glad we didn't have to waste time picking the lock, as he had on his first trip there. We filed into what was yet another darkened space. A strong odour hit me as I entered, making my eyes water. It was like vinegar, peat and lye all rolled into one. I swore it made the hairs in my nostrils shrivel.

A muffled gagging sound came from knee height.

'What in the seven seas is that *stench*?' Klous said.

'That would be General Frobisher,' Grub said, grinning, although his own eyes had taken on a distinctly watery sheen.

'Never mind weed killer,' Klous choked. 'By the smell of that stuff, it could take out the kraken!'

'For all our sake, let's hope you're right,' said Mrs Winchester. 'Right, everyone, look around. Let's see if we can't get some sort of light going.'

'Hang on.'

There was a brief pause and then a match flared, the bright spark of light making me blink. When I recovered, the room was filled with a weak yellow light and Grub was standing before us holding a candle, complete with holder.

'Stashed it here last time, in case I needed to come back,' he said, grinning.

'What could possibly have made you think coming back would be likely?' I asked.

He looked uncomfortable. 'Well, truthfully, I thought maybe I'd be able to sell some of this stuff.' He waved an arm at the rows and rows of glass demijohns that filled the room. They lined the walls, filled half the floor, and covered the entire surface of a large wooden table at the back of the space. 'I thought–'

A loud groan cut him off.

We all froze. What could be groaning in the damp cellar of a monster-haunted mansion? Whatever it was, I was pretty certain I didn't want to meet it.

A shadow shifted under the table. Slowly, I bent my knees to get a better look.

'Mr Gout!' I exclaimed, relief rushing through my veins. My master was slowly rolling out from under the table. He looked dishevelled, his nice suit stained and torn in a dozen places. There was a nasty cut above his left eye. He groaned again and got unsteadily to his knees. I rushed over to help, grabbing a large arm and helping to haul him to his feet. Mrs Winchester was a step behind me, fussing around him like a hen, swatting away some of the dust and cobwebs he'd picked up from the floor.

'You ridiculous man, just look at the state of you!' she scolded.

He turned to look at her, struggling to focus and swaying alarmingly. I tugged at his arm to keep him balanced.

'Ridiculous?' he said. 'Yes...yes, I suppose so. Where are we, exactly?'

'Near the cellar,' Grub said, helpfully.

Mr Gout stared at him. 'And who might you be?'

'This is Grub,' I said. 'He helped us get in and find you.'

'Did you indeed? Well, my thanks, my boy. Yes...yes my thanks indeed.'

He turned his bleary eyes on me. 'And who are you?'

PART NINE

My heart sank. 'W...what?'

'I'm so sorry. Have we already been introduced? You must excuse me, I'm feeling a little...well, a little something.'

'It's finally happened!' Klous squawked. 'He's finally cracked!'

Mr Gout looked at him, eyes bulging. 'My word, a talking frog!'

'Theo, what's the last thing you remember?' Mrs Winchester asked, her hands still brushing compulsively at his waistcoat. He appeared not to hear her, but then looked down with raised eyebrows.

'I'm so sorry. Are you talking to me, my good woman?'

'What?'

'You mentioned a Theo?'

'That's you!' Mrs Winchester squeaked, looking truly alarmed now.

Mr Gout gazed at her. 'Theo...' he said, trying

the word out in his mouth like a foreign language. 'Can't say it rings a bell, but I'll take your word for it.' There was a loud gurgling sound from the vicinity of his stomach. He clapped his hand to it and said, 'My word, but I'm absolutely famished! I don't suppose this place has a kitchen, does it?'

'He hasn't forgotten his stomach,' Klous said, rolling his enormous eyes.

Grub was looking on nervously. 'Is…is he alright?'

Mrs Winchester scowled at him. 'Don't be daft, boy. Does he sound alright to you? Bloody fool has completely forgotten who he is!'

Mr Gout scratched his chin, looking thoughtful. 'Do you know, I think you might be right. How…strange, I suppose. Although that description hardly seems adequate.' He thought some more.

'Very strange,' he added.

'Do you think it's the curse?' I asked the room at large.

Mr Gout raised an eyebrow. 'Curse? What a peculiar notion. I think someone has been reading too many novels. It's quite simple. I must have hit my head or something. I'm sure things will be right as rain in no time.'

It was at this point that the universe displayed an absolutely perfect understanding of dramatic tension. Something hit the door from the outside, making it rattle in its frame.

Grub winced. 'I think it's found us!'

'It?' Mr Gout asked, eyebrow raised.

There was another thump, and the sound of something slithering on the floor in the corridor.

His other eyebrow joined the first.

'This...will be a little complicated to explain,' I said. 'And we don't have time, anyway. Just trust us when we say we need to be ready when that door breaks down.'

Mr Gout's eyes bulged. 'Breaks down! Oh, my...'

Thump. Rattle. Slither. Thump.

'And, er, was there some sort of plan?'

'Weed killer,' said Klous with grim cheerfulness.

Mr Gout looked at him. 'I really must have given the ole noggin a good whack,' he said, raising his hands to his head, running them over as if checking for lumps.

'We don't have time for you, you useless lump,' Mrs Winchester said, a little harshly, elbowing him out of the way.

'How exactly are we planning to do this?' I asked nervously. 'Just chuck it at the monster or what?'

Thump. Rattle.

'Unless you have a better idea?' said Mrs Winchester, glaring at a bottle of weed killer as she attempted to hump it off the table. It slipped from her grasp and fell, smashing on the stone floor with a loud crash and a spray of murky green liquid. A few drops hit me in the face and immediately stung. The widening pool on the floor steamed and bubbled, giving off a powerful and eye-watering smell of rotten cabbages, vinegar and something undefinable. We all took a collective step back.

'I'm terribly sorry, but did you say *monster*?' Mr Gout asked, staring at the mess. His face had gone a little pale.

'Technically, we think it's a petunia,' I said. 'Only it's grown rather bigger than normal.'

Slither, thump, rattle, slither.

'A petunia?' he said weakly. 'I see.'

Rattle, rattle, rattle, THUMP.

'Err…how much bigger, exactly?'

'Have you ever seen a Venus flytrap?' Grub asked.

'Um…yes.'

'We're the flies.'

'Ah… Is it at all possible that I've gone mad?'

'Entirely, you great buffoon,' Mrs Winchester said, heaving another bottle off the table, carefully avoiding stepping in the remains of the first. I rushed to help her. 'But unless we find a way out of here, you'll be dead *and* mad!'

'This is all rather upsetting,' he said, but grabbed another bottle anyway. He lifted it off the table with apparent ease, but seemed at a loss for what to do with it once he had.

Grub heaved another off the table and staggered towards the door with it. 'Well, I suggest we start by dousing the door. Not sure how much it will help, but it's a start.'

The three of us set to, while Klous, being too small to carry one of the bottles, searched for another exit. By the time we had splashed the door and a goodly portion of the surrounding wall and floor with the horrible General Frobisher's, he returned, looking grim.

'We're stuffed,' he said. 'Only one way out and one way in.'

'Is there any way you can... I don't know, chuck this stuff at it as it comes through? Hit it like you did before, but this time with the weed killer too?'

The little creature glowered at me darkly. 'What am I, a magical gardener?'

'Can you or can't you?' Mrs Winchester snapped.

There was a loud smash and the door visibly gave way a little, bits of plaster drifting down from where the hinges were being slowly driven from the wall.

Klous gulped. 'Well, telekinesis ain't really my thing, but I'll tell you what, I'll give it a bloody good go!' He threw out his little clawed hands, bowed his head, and screwed up his face in concentration.

Nothing happened.

The door shook again under another colossal attack.

'Um...how's it going?' I asked.

'I said it wasn't my thing!' Klous wailed.

Another smash, this time leaving the door visibly splintered. It wouldn't hold out much longer.

'Bugger this,' said Klous, dropping his arms. 'I'm going to try something else.' He squatted down like a toad, placing his hands against the flagstone floor, carefully avoiding the wet patches.

'What exactly?'

'I'm a bloody Kobold, ain't I?' he screeched in response. He had his eyes screwed shut and a look of intense concentration on his face.

'Oh lord, he's trying to take possession of the castle,' Mrs Winchester said, a look of awe on her face.

'How do you mean?' Grub asked.

'He's a Kobold,' she said, as if explaining something simple to the dreadfully dull. 'That's what they do. They take magical possession of a property. A kind of ownership. That's how they get such a hold, why they're so hard to get rid of. Only...'

'What?'

'Well, Klous is a Klabautermann...a sea Kobold. He takes ships. I don't think he's ever taken possession of a house before, let alone one this size!'

I looked at him. He was obviously concentrating very hard on something, although the only visible manifestation of that was the beads of sweat breaking out all across his little warty face.

'I don't understand any of this!' Mr Gout wailed as the door shook for what must surely be the last time before it gave way entirely.

'If I end up ate by a bloody bedding plant, I'll be paying you a visit in the afterwards, Theophilius, you great, useless prune!' Mrs Winchester screeched, brandishing a half-full bottle of General Frobisher's as the door finally gave way with an almighty crash and an explosion of plaster dust.

Coughing and spluttering, I tried to wave away the fine powder from my face. I could just make out long tentacle-like vines shooting into the room. Some grabbed the doorframe, as if using it as an anchor from which to pull some obscured bulk further forward. But then they let go almost immediately, flinching back as if they'd been burned. Indeed, I swore I could hear a fine sizzling sound as the plant's flesh met the sticky, drenched wood.

'It works!' I choked out, my throat burning and my eyes gritty and stinging.

Mrs Winchester gave a yell and heaved her bottle at the thing. It smashed to the floor at the base of the doorway, splashing the foul liquid up over the thrashing tentacles, which hissed where it touched them and shrank back.

'That won't hold it for long!' she shouted above the noise.

'How's it coming, Klous?' I cried.

The Kobold hadn't moved. He shook his

head, eyes closed. 'So…big. Need… more…time,' he managed.

A vine shot out at Mr Gout, who shrieked and dropped the bottle he'd been carrying. Luckily, it smashed and the flying spray it produced was enough to hold back the vine long enough for him to dodge away. Grub followed it up with two rolled jars, their tops open, spilling their contents freely across the floor. It kept the vines from touching the flagstones, but not from moving through the air. Three shot out of the centre of the doorway directly at me. I dodged two, but the third found a hold around my right wrist. It almost yanked me from my feet, pulling me towards the open doorway.

'Klous!' I yelled.

'I…I can't do it! It's just too big…'

'Right, Plan B!' Mrs Winchester cried, launching herself at the vine that held me. Something flashed in her hand as she brought it down on the vine in a sweeping arc. It severed where she struck it, sending me sprawling backwards as the tension released and I landed painfully on the cold stone floor. The end of the vine still clung to my arm, stinging where it touched, thrashing like an eel. I hurried to prise it off, flinging it to one side and looking up to see Mrs Winchester standing over me, a large kitchen knife in her hand.

'Where did you get that?'

She looked momentarily guilty. 'The hotel,'

she admitted. 'I wasn't about to come in here unarmed after last time!'

I struggled to my feet and cursed myself for not doing something similar.

'What exactly is Plan B?' Grub asked, narrowly avoiding another vine as it snapped at his elbow.

'Jolly good question, lad!' Mr Gout cried, upending a bottle of General Frobisher's on the offending tentacle. 'I don't know what's going on here, or where here is, or who you people are, or who I am, or why we're being attacked by the shrubbery, but I do know that we're sitting ducks!'

'Well, thank you for stating the obvious!' Mrs Winchester said acidly. 'We'd none of us be in this situation if it wasn't for you and your pig-headedness!'

Mr Gout bristled. 'Madam, I assure you this has absolutely nothing to do with me!'

'This is your house, you bloody fool!'

'My good woman–'

'Don't you good woman me–'

'I hope you're not suggesting I keep dangerous plant life in my basement!'

'I should think that's the least of what you keep in your basement, you h–'

'Enough!' I shouted. 'This isn't helping.'

They both gaped at me but stopped squabbling.

'We need to get out of here. Mr Gout is right about that, at least. So suggestions, anyone? Klous, can you do any of those fireballs like last time?'

He glowered up at me. 'Now you want fire?! Give me a bloody minute to recover, will yer!'

'Alright. No fireballs.' I looked at the pool of weed killer spreading across the floor. 'Does this stuff burn, do you think?'

'Are you mad?' said Grub. 'Set light to this lot and the whole place will go up. You might kill the plant, but you'd take out most of the town with it – not to mention us, of course!'

'Then suggest something!' I cried, jumping out of the way of a seeking tentacle.

'You're the ones who are supposed to be the paranormal experts!' he retorted, batting the vine away with an empty bottle.

It was at this point that Custard hopped through the wall.

He appeared in the small room, sniffed at the pooling General Frobisher's, wrinkled up his nose in what can only have been disgust, then sat back on his rump and began washing his ears.

'Where have you been?' Mrs Winchester said accusingly. The rabbit ignored her.

Mr Gout was staring at him, his mouth a large O. 'Is…is that rabbit…?'

'Dead?' I said. 'Yes. Only he's come back. As a poltergeist. He's called Custard. He's yours.'

'My what?'

'Your pet.'

'I have a dead rabbit called Custard as a pet?'

'Yes.'

'This is all a lot for a man to take,' he said weakly.

'Where did he come from, anyway? Wasn't he with Obsidian?' Grub said, looking around worriedly, as if he expected the very alive cat to also appear out of one of the walls.

Then I had an idea.

'Your notebook!' I cried, racing to Mr Gout's side.

'I beg your pardon?'

'It should be in your jacket pocket. There might be something in it that can help us,' I elaborated.

He patted himself down, found a rectangular lump in his right breast pocket and produced the battered, leather-clad book. 'This?' he said uncertainly, looking at the thing as if it might explode.

I snatched it from him, deciding there was no time for niceties, and began flicking through the pages, searching desperately for anything that looked like it might be useful.

'Don't waste your time, girl,' Mrs Winchester said. 'Even if you found something, you'd never get it to work. You've never done magic before.'

'First time for everything,' I muttered, glancing over a page that seemed to describe in detail the digestive system of something called a chupacabra.

There seemed to be at least some sort of system to the notes. They were arranged under tatty tabs, giving the letters of the alphabet. The trouble was, I had no idea what I was looking for, let alone what letter I might find it under. Grub glanced over my shoulder.

'Try P for Petunia.'

'Don't be ridiculous!'

'Just trying to help!'

I ignored him, rifling through the pages, taking in a hundred different things that, in any other situation, probably would have fascinated me for hours. But right now, I needed a miracle. I was just considering looking under M when a title at the top of a page caught my eye.

Portal Spell

I scanned the page quickly.

There was a lot of information there. Information I didn't have time to read. A few words did pop out at me. Extremely dangerous, for example. And only use in an absolute emergency. Well, as far as I was concerned, this certainly qualified! At the bottom of the page was written what appeared to be an incantation. I couldn't understand a word of it. It was in Latin, although I didn't realise it at the time. I began to despair. How could I hope to produce any magic if I couldn't even understand the words?

I had to try.

I threw out my hand towards the many vines snaking out from the doorway, in a manner in which I had seen Mr Gout do when casting spells. Then I began to read.

'Eice me hinc, exi me ocyus hinc.
Ire celeriter debeo, satis fix sum.
Aperi ianuam, non curo quo adeat.
Vita vel mors est, nil aliud possum.'

I pronounced the words as best as I could guess. I know now how embarrassingly wrong I got it. But apparently that didn't matter, because the effect was immediate, alarming, and not quite as expected.

A small, swirling ring of purplish-grey smoke appeared around my feet. It quickly expanded, streaming outwards until it encompassed all of us.

Then the floor disappeared. Literally. It just…vanished.

And we fell.

I screamed. I'm pretty sure someone else did too, but it was hard to tell. The world rushed past my face at what felt like impossible speeds. Then I hit something hard and my feet went out from under me, knocking the breath from my body. I lay still for a moment, eyes tightly closed, my head spinning.

Someone groaned.

'Are we dead?'

I think that was Klous.

'Death doesn't hurt this much.'

That was definitely Mrs Winchester.

'Is…is everyone alright?' I managed.

'Define alright,' Mr Gout groaned.

I opened my eyes and rolled over, trying to take in where we were.

It seemed to be some sort of basement. Damp-looking stone walls surrounded us, green with moss or lichen. It was dark, but not pitch black, so light was getting in from somewhere.

There was no sign of the plant or its horrible vines.

'What happened?'

'What happened? What happened! You just did the impossible, my girl. That's what happened! That shouldn't have worked,' Mrs Winchester said, scrambling to her feet awkwardly and attempting to brush down her dress.

'I just said what it said in the book. Admittedly, I didn't expect it to open a portal beneath us, which seems like a bit of a flaw, but we did technically escape.'

'You could have killed us all!'

'We're fine,' I said, bristling a little. I had got us out of a sticky situation, after all. And I hadn't seen anyone else coming up with any good ideas.

'It shouldn't have worked,' she repeated.

'Why not?' I snapped.

'Because you don't just pick up a spell, sound it out and hey presto, magic! It doesn't work that way. It takes time, training. It...it just shouldn't have worked...' she trailed off.

'Well, it did,' I said. 'I suggest we move on and figure out where we are exactly, and what we're going to do next.' I took stock of my companions.

Klous was up and hopping about agitatedly. Mr Gout was sitting on his behind, looking dazed. Mrs Winchester was glaring at me like I'd just professed to devil worship, while Grub was the only one not to have moved yet. Custard was sniffing around him with interest.

'You alright, Grub?' I asked, crawling up to him.

'This is mad,' he said, eyes still closed. 'Utterly mad. You people are mad.' He opened his eyes and grinned at me. 'I love it!' he finished. I couldn't help but grin back.

He was kind of right. This was mad, but, well, I had to admit it was pretty amazing too. I had just done magic. I thought about what my mother would have said about that. I'm sure she would have found some way to make it seem like a personal failing.

I shook myself. No time for that now. I looked around.

We must be in the castle's basement, or some sort of sub-basement. Wasn't that where the plant was supposed to be? I looked around in the gloom, shivering a little, imagining those vines snaking out of the shadows at me. But clearly, we were currently alone. Wherever the monster was, it wasn't here. I looked up at the ceiling, but whatever portal I had created was gone now. I realised we were lucky Custard was with us; his green-blue glow illuminated the dank room. There was no other light source. Looking more closely, I realised there were shadowy shapes in the corners of the room. Crates, perhaps; some kind of storage. Was this a storeroom? If so, there must be a way out.

'Custard!' I called, beckoning the bunny over. He hopped towards me, bringing his ghostly light with him, illuminating additional parts of our environment. There seemed to be some sort of passage leading out through an empty doorway ahead of us. It seemed as good a direction as any.

'Shall we go?' I asked.

'Go where?' asked Grub, groaning as he got to his feet.

'Well, that's a good question. We need to decide if we're looking for a way out, or if we're going to confront that thing again.'

Mr Gout, now standing, gasped. 'Confront it? Are you mad, girl? Why on earth would we want to do that? Surely we should get out of here!'

'You're the one who came in here looking for a fight,' I pointed out.

He whitened. 'I didn't...did I?'

'I'm afraid so. Against our advice, I might add.'

'Oh dear, oh dear.... Do you know, I don't understand myself at all.'

'Join the club,' Mrs Winchester grumbled. 'Whatever we're doing, we can't stay here.'

'Follow the rabbit then, I guess?' suggested

Grub.

I nodded. 'Follow the rabbit.'

#

It did little for any of our nerves, I think, following a dead rabbit's ghostly glow down the dank corridors of Castle Gout's underbelly. I couldn't decide if it was a blessing or a curse that so little was illuminated as we passed. It left the imagination to play with the shadowy shapes, but who knew if that wasn't better than seeing clearly what might be lurking down here. It was wet, smelly, and I had so far counted at least three different types of mushrooms growing in the cracks and crevices of the sub-basement. I couldn't help but wonder what on earth this place had been built for, originally.

'You bring me to all the nicest places,' Klous muttered as we squelched through a patch of what we were all fervently hoping was mud. As a group, we ignored him.

'So,' Grub whispered, coming up beside me so that we were walking close together. 'Do you do this sort of thing often?'

I turned to look at his face, pale blue in the ghostly light. 'This may shock you,' I said. 'But no.'

'Well alright, so not exactly this,' he amended. 'But this sort of thing?'

'Honestly, until a few months ago, I would have laughed at anyone who tried to tell me that any of this was actually real. But lately…yes, I do this sort of thing all the time!' I admitted.

'Was that really the first time you've done magic?' he asked next.

'Yes.'

'Why did the old woman tell you it shouldn't have worked?'

'I'm sure I don't know,' I said, a little stiffly. 'Clearly she was wrong.'

'Well, it was very impressive.'

'Um, thank you,' I said, a blush creeping to my cheeks. Why did that *keep* happening? I tried to pull away from the boy, but he followed, apparently not done with his questions.

'Are we really going to destroy the monster?'

'I don't know,' I said. 'At this point, I'd be happy just to see the sky again. But we need to break my master's curse, so I suppose we'll have to face it, eventually.'

'This curse…what is it exactly?'

I paused, unsure what I should share, but then I figured Grub had probably seen enough by this time to make keeping secrets pointless. 'Well, for a start, it took his memory. He spent many years unsure of his life from before. Where he came from, what happened to him. He's only recently pieced parts of it together.'

'Like the location of this place?'

'Right. Then there's the sleeping thing…'

'What? He can't *sleep*?' Grub sounded horrified by the very idea.

'No, he can sleep just fine, only he can't sleep under any sort of permanent roof. One meant for human habitation, anyway. He just lies awake, apparently. So he has to sleep in caravans, tents, stables – that sort of thing.'

Grub was silent for a while, then asked, 'Why on earth would anybody bother to curse someone with *that*?'

'I don't know. But when you add it to the loss of his memories and his home, I think the curse was designed to strip him of everything he had... everything he was.'

Grub gave a low whistle. 'He must have really got on somebody's wrong side!'

I gave a grim smile in the darkness. 'It's the sort of thing he does.'

Our conversation stopped when Custard halted at a sort of crossroads in the passages. His little ghostly nose twitched at each option, but he seemed unable to decide which way to go.

'Now what?' Klous asked.

I shrugged. 'I guess we have to choose.'

There were three passages, not including the one we'd just come down. Each looked exactly the same: featureless, dark, and pregnant with the possibility of death or escape. I had no idea which direction to choose. As it happened, the choice was made for us.

Somebody screamed.

I whipped my head around in time to see Mr Gout pulled to the ground by the thickest vine I had yet seen, which shot out of the shadows from the right-hand passage and wrapped itself around one of his ankles. No sooner was he on the ground then another three vines appeared, fastening around his legs and arms, then pulling him with shocking speed across the dirt floor and back down the passage from which they had emerged.

'*Help!*' he cried, struggling uselessly. '*Help...* HELP!'

Mrs Winchester, the closest to him, grabbed at him, but caught only air. Klous bounded after him, but he too fell short. My master disappeared into the darkness before I could move more than one step.

Without discussion, we gave chase. I scooped up Custard, and we tore after him.

'That plant really wants your boss!' Grub shouted.

'It's probably the whole reason it's here!' I shouted back. 'To stop him from breaking the curse!'

'Well then, it's a good job we're here!'

I wish I had his confidence. 'This is bad!' I yelled to Mrs Winchester. 'We could run right into a trap!'

'I agree,' she replied, panting with exertion. 'But the only other choice is to just let the plant take him and we have no idea what could happen then!'

There was a sudden welling of orange light as Klous, still jumping along beside us, readied a fireball between his clawed hands.

'I gotta learn that trick!' Grub grunted.

Mr Gout's wails were still coming back to us down the corridor, but they were fainter and fainter. However fast we were following, it seemed he was moving faster. Then suddenly I couldn't hear him at all. I swore under my breath and urged my legs to go faster.

A tiny glow of white light appeared in the distance.

'What's that?'

'It looks like...daylight!' Grub said.

'Alright, stop...*stop*!' I cried, throwing my arms out to slow the rest of them with me as I stumbled to a walk. 'We can't just go charging in. Let's at least try to get a look at what we're dealing with before we run right into it. Klous, you're our main weapon here. If you see a good shot, take it.'

'Yes, marm,' he said, the fireball still spinning and growing between his hands.

'You two,' I continued. 'Well...just be ready.'

Grub nodded silently, looking pale. Mrs Winchester looked as though she might argue, but then changed her mind. 'Very well. What are you going to do?'

'I'm going to do whatever I can,' I said. I pulled Mr Gout's notebook out from the front of my dress where I'd stashed it after our fall.

Mrs Winchester pursed her lips, but nodded. 'Just...for god's sake, be careful!'

The light in the distance was growing larger

as we approached; it did indeed look like light streaming in through a window. But how could that be? I'd assumed we were well below ground level.

We came to a corner in the passage. Whatever the light was, it was emanating from around it. I took a moment to make sure everyone was ready, and then, as one, we stepped around the corner.

PART TEN

The room was low-ceilinged. So low, in fact, Grub had to stoop to stop his head bumping against the stone. The shadows were thick at the corners, but a disturbing scene was etched out before us in the white light coming from some sort of shaft in the ceiling. What we saw was a monstrous mass of writhing tentacles, or vines. They snaked out across the floor in all directions from the centre of the room where...

How to describe it?

It was a flower. A magenta, trumpet-shaped flower, much like the one I had seen with Grub in the abandoned greenhouse, earlier that morning and a hundred years ago.

But that doesn't sound right at all. That sounds delicate, pretty. It was neither of those things. It was a gigantic funnel-shaped thing, like an elongated, hooded head, which, unnervingly, turned to face us as we entered. Inside, the opening looked wet and dark. I decided I would do literally anything to stay as far away from it as possible. Unfortunately, that would not be an option, because Mr Gout's prostrate form was slumped upside down directly beneath the wavering flower. His two thick legs were sticking up in the air at odd angles, his trouser legs rolling down to reveal white ankles and calves. He was clearly out cold. Again. Never mind the curse, the poor man was in danger of serious brain injury at this rate.

Without discussion, Klous launched his fireball directly at the hooded head. The thing lurched to the side to avoid it, but clearly had little movement, rooted as it was by a short trunk, or stem, thicker than Mr Gout's middle, into the earthen floor. Unfortunately, one of the large vines whipped up to meet the projectile and blocked the shot. It suffered heavy damage, but the head was unharmed.

Klous cursed and began forming another fireball between his hands.

I decided not to wait. Carrying the blade Mrs Winchester had passed to me in one hand and the notebook in the other, I darted towards Mr Gout's prostrate form. I stumbled over vine after vine, which rolled and slithered beneath the soles of my boots most unpleasantly. Vines whipped at my face and grabbed at my ankles, but I evaded them with quick steps and some wild flailing with the knife. I even batted one away with a vicious strike from the notebook. I was aware of Mrs Winchester, slicing and dicing her way through vine after vine, wielding two more knives that she had produced from somewhere about her person. Another fireball flew over my head and was snatched out of the air by a vine that had been heading for my head. I was getting closer to the flower. It swivelled to face me and I almost turned tail and ran when a great guttural moaning began emanating from deep within it. No plant life should have been able to make noises like that. Mr Gout was still not moving. I hoped we weren't already too late.

Something flashed in the corner of my vision and I turned just in time to see a thick vine hit me in the side of the head, knocking me from my feet. I rolled to a stop in the dirt, head spinning and little lights flashing before my eyes. I cried out as something grabbed me around my left forearm, biting into the flesh. As my vision cleared, I could see a vine gripped tightly me, and others were approaching fast.

I guess it was now or never.

As we'd walked the dim underground corridors, I had taken a few moments to flip through my master's book. I hadn't really wanted to try another untested spell, figuring I'd probably got lucky with the portal. But I wanted to be prepared in case I had no other option.

Well, I'm pretty sure I had no other option.

The monster was just too powerful. At this rate, it would either kill us, or at the very least drive us off before we'd rescued Mr Gout. And I had found a spell that sounded...well, it sounded like, if I pulled it off, it might just work.

I flipped open the book to the page I'd marked earlier and began to recite the words, words that once again I could not hope to understand.

> *'Virtutem terrae invoco.*
> *aufer a te quod ablatum est.*
> *Exsuge id, quod ti–'*

I was cut short when another vine snapped around my free arm, gripping it tight and yanking, making me drop the book. A third vine whipped towards me and fastened around my waist. I gasped, the air rushing from my mouth as it tightened, and I was powerless to stop it. I was now being dragged towards the monstrous flower. I looked frantically for the notebook and found it lying face up on the floor just a foot or two away. It was even still open on the right page.

But I had no way of getting to it. And as I was pulled away, I felt any chance of our success slipping away, too.

But then I realised I didn't need the book. I just needed to read it.

I started reciting again, my eyes already desperately scanning ahead, ahead to parts I hadn't managed before.

> *'Virtutem terrae invoco.*

aufer a te quod ablatum est.
Exsuge id, quod tibi victui est spoliandum.'

I stopped. There was one more line of text, but I couldn't quite make it out. But it was only getting smaller...only getting further away. I'd just have to do my best.

'Quod vitam dedit, nunc tibi reddatur.'

At first I thought nothing had happened. But then the vines holding me gave a sort of shudder and the pitch of the plant's moaning grew higher and louder. I felt the thing's grip on me loosen.

'Nice work!' Grub called from the other side of the room.

The plant's thick stem was now shaking back and the forth, and although the many vines still thrashed through the air, there seemed less intention behind their movement.

'What the hell did you just do?'

Mrs Winchester was approaching me through the furiously moving vines, shoving them aside as she stalked towards me.

'Earth magic...I think.'

'*You think*?!' Her face was furious. 'Do you know how dangerous that was?'

I stood my ground. 'Less dangerous than doing nothing. I just asked the earth to...to take back what it had given to the plant.'

'*You don't know that*!' she screeched. 'You

have no idea what you're doing. Magic is dangerous. It's volatile. You...you shouldn't even be able to do it!'

'*Why not?*' I snapped back.

'You...you just shouldn't.' Her response was almost mumbled. She had stopped a few feet away from me and the fire seemed to have gone out of her. Instead, she was staring at me with an expression I couldn't read.

'Well, I can,' I said coolly. 'And it seems to be working.' I threw up a hand towards the huge flower head, which was now definitely quaking, shaking from side to side as the stem below it seemed to be shrinking, collapsing in on itself. The vines had now mostly fallen to the ground, but were still wriggling and twitching like worms on the earth.

She glowered at me. 'Oh, it's working, is it? And what, exactly, is it doing?'

'You've no idea! How could you?' she continued when I tried to think of a response.

She was right, of course. I had no idea what the spell was doing, not really. I only knew the little information that had been hastily scrawled in Mr Gout's notebook. I knew it was an earth spell. It was supposed to, as far as I could work out, suck back out of a plant all the energy it had taken from the soil. At first I'd wondered about what possible use such a spell would be in normal circumstances. But then I realised I knew of several farmers back home who would have paid handsomely to have an entire field cleared of all weeds with the speed the monster seemed to shrink back.

The vines had all shrivelled up now. They looked like dozens of thin black strings coming out of the main stalk, which itself was now brown and withered. Even the flower was browning and crinkled around the edge of the petals. Ignoring Mrs Winchester, I went to check on Mr Gout. I felt down beside him and placed one hand on his chest. He groaned and opened his eyes.

'Oh, it's you,' he said. 'Miss Truddle, right?'

I sighed. 'Miss Trussel. Are you alright? Do you think you can get up?' I helped the man slowly to his feet.

'Now what?' This was from Grub.

'Now,' I said, as I watched the flower head collapse in on itself. 'Now we have a hex bag to find. It's the source of the curse,' I explained before he could open his mouth to ask. 'And something tells me this plant was put here to protect it.'

'Alright. And what do we do once we've found it?'

I shrugged. 'We destroy it. Burning works; I know that much.'

Klous appeared at my side, a fireball hovering over one palm. 'Burning I can do,' he said.

I smiled weakly. 'Calm down, we have to find it first.'

'I think we just did.' Klous pointed a clawed finger at the desiccated remains of the petunia's main stem. It had completely dried out now, and a large split ran down the papery skin, revealing a hollow space inside in which sat a small hessian sack tied with string. It had a green lily stamped on it. I cocked an eyebrow at Mrs Winchester, who took a look. She nodded, once.

'Burn it,' I said to Klous.

The Kobold didn't so much throw the fireball as place it gently on top of the little hex bag.

'We should probably stand well back,' I said, remembering that the last hex bag I'd seen had exploded.

All five of us – six if you counted Custard, who I now held in my arms – gathered at the entrance to the little room, well away from harm, and waited.

'What exactly are we doing?' Mr Gout leant down and asked into my ear.

'You'll see soon enough,' I said, adding, 'Hopefully.'

I watched as the large man straightened up, staring at the little fire in the middle of the room with a mixture of confusion and worry. Then, slowly, his expression changed. The befuddled look slipped away, and although the worry remained, or even increased, in his expression, the slightly dazed nature of his gaze disappeared, to be replaced with a flinty countenance. Tears began to well in his eyes.

'Are…are you alright?'

'I remember,' he said.

'What? What do you remember?'

'So many things,' he whispered.

'Yeah, yeah, great, we broke the curse,' Klous said, bouncing with nervous energy. 'Now, how are we gonna find our way out of here? 'Cos I don't know about you lot, but I ain't got a clue.'

Grub looked over my shoulder and smiled. 'I think I have the solution to that.'

I turned to see Obsidian sat in the middle of the corridor, apparently completely unconcerned, quietly licking one of his paws.

'This time we follow the cat,' I said.

#

I stood blinking in the bright afternoon sun. We had been in the bowels of Castle Gout for longer than I had realised. Birds were calling from the trees. The light rustle of leaves was brought down to me by the slightest of breezes. There was a sweet spring smell on the air.

Mr Gout stood next to me, hands clasped behind his back, bouncing up and down on the balls of his feet. He was silent, staring out across the rolling hills, but I could feel he was building up to something. I was content to wait. The air and heat from the sun were nice on my skin. I felt...different. Not in a way I could really put into words. But something had changed in me, down in the sub-basement of the Gouts' ancestral home. I was not the Clementine Trussel who had entered the night before. This was something I needed to examine...but not yet. For now, I was at a strange sort of peace. I waited for Mr Gout to arrive at whatever thought he was formulating in that unfathomable head of his.

When he did finally speak, he didn't turn to look at me, but kept staring out over the Devon landscape, as if searching for something in the far distance.

'Miss Trussel, there is much about my life I did not tell you when we first met,' he said. 'Perhaps I should have. Or perhaps this was the way things would always have unfolded. Whatever the case, I cannot undo that now. All I can do is beg your forgiveness. I am old, older than I look, as I'm sure you have by this time figured out. Sometimes I feel every one of those years, even if I'm unsure exactly how many there are.'

He paused. I stayed silent, letting him think.

'The curse is lifted. I have to say it is a peculiar feeling, after all this time. I have lived my life for so many years in a sort of fog; one that obscured many things from me, but that also, after a time, became so very familiar. Now the vapours have cleared and I see more clearly than I have in decades. I finally know, truly, who I am. And where I have been.'

He paused again, heaving a great sigh. I hardly dared breathe, unless some movement from me might distract his chain of thought.

'Yes,' he began again. 'Much is clear to me now, and yet still not everything. It is as though I have unlocked a strongbox, only to find a smaller, tougher one inside. I know who I am, and I know where I have been, but I do not know *why*. That perhaps I could live with. If I have learnt anything in my long years, it is that not every mystery must be explained. But this one, I fear, I must yet uncover. For it concerns not just myself...but also you, my dear Clementine.'

'M...me?' I blurted out in surprise. Mr Gout turned to look at me then, and his blue eyes seemed older than they ever had before.

'Yes, my dear. You. For you did something today that you should not have been able to do. And I must admit that I fear for what it means.'

'The spells? The portal? And...and what I did to the petunia? All I did was read the words from your notebook. I'm sure it was just beginner's luck.'

He smiled at me sadly. 'I wish that were so. You are, after all, a most remarkable young woman. I had meant to teach you many things about my craft. I fear that thus far I have not been the best teacher, but you have thrived in this life nonetheless. But one thing I never meant to teach you, my dear, was magic.'

'Y...you didn't?' I said, surprised. 'But I thought–'

'That you were my apprentice? Indeed, and no doubt, I should have been clearer about what that position did, and did not, mean. You are my apprentice, and, should you still desire it after today, I will continue to teach you everything I can about the paranormal and this world I have dragged you into. But my dear, I did not mean the performing of spells to be one of those things, for the simple reason that it should have been impossible for you to perform them. That itself was a piece of knowledge I had meant to impart. You see magic...magic is not something that humans can do.'

'So...that would make you...'

'Not human. Not entirely, at any rate.'

I took a moment to let that sink in. No...it was going to take longer than a moment.

'I see,' I lied. 'And so, that would make me...?'

'Well, that's the question, my dear.'

'You might have mentioned you weren't human,' I said, a touch reproachfully.

He smiled. 'I daresay I might. However, it is not such an easy topic to broach, I think you'll find. Also, until today, all I had were suspicions.'

'I'm not sure I understand. Your parents... *My* parents–'

'Are entirely human, I have no doubt,' he hastened to say.

'Well then, how can you...how can *we* possibly be different?'

He sighed. 'I wish I could give you a straight answer. I really do. But as I said before, there are still parts of my own story I do not entirely understand. Still passages of time that I cannot account for. What I do know is this: I went somewhere. Somewhere that is not *here*.' He waved his hands around to indicate, I felt not just the castle and grounds, but the world in general. 'While I was gone, I was changed. Quite how, I cannot say. But I came back *different*. My age, for one thing. I was born in 1825, which should make me eighty years old. I flatter myself by saying that I do not look eighty. Then there is the magic. To the best of my knowledge, I never performed a single spell before I disappeared. It was only on my return that I gained that ability.'

My mind was racing. I tried to fathom what he was telling me. 'So...' I said slowly. 'If going to this place, wherever it was, gave you the ability to do magic, are you saying I must have been there as well? Because I have to say I think I'd remember...' I trailed off. Would I? Would I remember something like that happening to me? Mr Gout hadn't. Still didn't, not properly. So was it possible? No, surely not. Even if I didn't remember, my family certainly would have noticed if I disappeared. Wouldn't they?

'I have a headache,' I said eventually.

'I've no doubt,' said Mr Gout.

'Just to be clear, are you saying we've both been...to the same place, wherever, *whatever* that might be?'

'To be honest, my dear, I do not know. It could be that two entirely separate events befell us.

However, we must consider your grandmother.'

'Granny? Don't tell me she's not human either!'

'Ah-ha, no, fear not. I believe she is, also, one hundred per cent *Homo sapiens*. But I am thinking about our very first meeting, my dear.'

'The Alp.'

'Yes. Stephen. Your grandmother's former lover, turned into a beast by–'

'By the Green Lily!' I finished for him. The same person, or people, who cursed you!'

'So it would seem.'

'And you still don't remember who they are?'

'I do not. However, we now have clues. The Hams, to their misfortune, saw me the day I was cursed.'

'They saw you fall out of a portal. Was it like the one I cast, do you think?'

'Perhaps. But I suspect it was, forgive me, a good deal more complex. If I were to theorise, I would say that they saw me reappearing in this world, from wherever I had been.'

'They saw a woman, too. Do you think that's who cursed you? Do you think she's the one who uses the green lily?'

'Perhaps.'

'But you don't remember any of that, do you?'

Mr Gout shook his head.

'So what is the first thing you *do* remember?'

He smiled at a memory. 'The first thing I

could recall was standing at the edge of a road in a very heavy thunderstorm. I made my way to an inn called, of all things, The Winking Duck. I believe the year was 1877.'

'Sounds nice.'

'Names can be deceiving. Anyway, I wouldn't recommend visiting. It burned down shortly after my arrival.'

'Gosh. You didn't…?'

'I was perhaps involved, though, I believe, not entirely at fault,' he admitted.

'That sort of thing does tend to happen when you're around. You have to admit,' I said.

He sniffed. 'I'm sure I don't know what you mean, my girl. But the point is, that is the first event I remember upon my return. I do not know how I got there. I do not know anything, really. Little pieces of my life slowly filled themselves in over the years that followed. Much quicker since we met.'

'What about from before you disappeared? What's the last thing you remember from back then?'

'That is a lot more hazy,' he said. 'I cannot really say, for sure.'

'What year was it? That might be a start. '

'1863, I believe. My brother passed away in 1841.'

'So you must have been gone for some time. No wonder you look so well preserved.'

'Indeed. The question is, how do *you* fit into

all this, my dear?'

'Well, I wasn't born until 1890.'

'Quite the conundrum, isn't it?'

'I can't make any sense of it,' I admitted with a small shrug.

'Well, it seems we do not have all the pieces of the puzzle yet. But I think we now know who does.'

'The woman who cursed you? But we don't know anything about her!'

'We know she uses the green lily,' he said. 'I think perhaps it is time for me to call up an old favour. I have a friend, an old friend, who might know where to find her.'

'You do? Why haven't you gone to them before now?'

'It is…complicated. That is all I will say for now. But the matter is now pressing enough to warrant a visit, I think.'

'When do we leave?'

He laughed. 'Give an old man a chance to acclimatise. Besides, don't you have a young man to tend to?' He raised a single eyebrow, his eyes twinkling.

I felt the all-too-familiar blush creep onto my cheeks. 'I…I don't know what you're talking about.'

'Quite so,' he replied with a smile. 'Nevertheless, I should be grateful if you would convey a message to young Mr Grub for me.'

'Oh. Alright. And I think it's just Grub.'

'Well Mr or no, I'd be grateful if you could let him know he is free to stay on the estate as long as he wishes. And that includes the inside of the house, not just the grounds. It's far too big to be left unused.'

'I'm sure he'll be happy to hear that. Are we…are we going to move in?'

'I haven't decided. Mrs Winchester has already intimated her desire to help me settle here, but I should hate to keep her from Oystercatcher Cottage. In fact, I think I'd rather miss the old place myself. And this house…' he turned to look back at his grand ancestral home. 'Holds mixed memories for me. How about you, my dear? If you do indeed plan to stick with me, do you have a preference for where we live?'

I looked back, too. 'I have to admit, I never thought I'd even have the option of living in a house like this.'

He smiled. 'It has its pros and cons, from what I remember. I'd have to think about staff. I do not know how many we would even need to run a house this size. When I was growing up…well, I admit, it was not something I ever really thought about. No doubt I should have.'

'Well,' I said. 'I think the decision must be yours, Mr Gout. I will be happy with whatever you decide.'

'Can I take that to mean you have forgiven me and intend to remain as my apprentice?'

I didn't meet his eyes. 'I cannot pretend that

I am not angry about what you have hidden from me,' I said. 'But I do not feel it is yet time for me to abandon this path. Now especially. So we will take one day at a time. How about that?'

He smiled again. 'A splendid suggestion, Miss Trussel.'

The End

Trussel and Gout will return in: Werewolves in the Kitchen, Vampire at the Door

Turn The Page For A Free Book!

GET YOUR FREE BOOK!

Sign Up To The M.a.knights
Vip Readers Club At

Www.maknightswrites.co.uk

And Get The Free Prequel Novella

BOOKS BY THIS AUTHOR

The Pig In The Derby Hat

Young Clementine Trussel didn't go looking for the supernatural. It found her.

When a small pig wearing a derby hat falls out of her Granny's window, Clementine is inclined to believe she's seeing things. Only someone else saw it too, the mysterious Theophilius Gout, and he claims to be an expert in the paranormal.

There is definitely something odd about the fat, tweed-clad man, and when her Granny falls deathly ill, Clementine is uneasy entrusting her recovery to a stranger. Even one as enigmatic as Mr Gout. Besides, he seems more interested in the cakes from her parents' bakery than anything... otherworldly.

But with her grandmother's life, and Clementine's own future, hanging in the balance, she is forced to follow him into a world of magic and monsters hidden in the shadows of her quiet hometown.

Will they be in time to save her Granny? Is Mr Gout

what he claims to be? And just what exactly is the pig in the derby hat?

Something In The Woodshed

Mr Gout had not told me everything.
That became clear the very first night I arrived to take up my position as his apprentice.

Paranormal investigation is not quite what Clementine Trussel was expecting. Abermwyl, the small Welsh fishing village she now calls home, is hardly a hub of excitement. Worse still, her welcome has been less than warm.

Mr Gout seems distracted, and his ancient housekeeper, one Mrs Winchester, has made it abundantly clear she is not happy with Clementine's presence.

But strange events are about to unfold in the sleepy village. A tragic shipwreck brings a mysterious stranger to shore. A madman. The sole survivor. But could the ship have brought something else with it, too?

Clementine cannot shake the feeling she is being watched, and, in the woodshed behind the cottage she now calls home, she feels a presence lurking.

The White Owl Of Thicklewood Hall

It's Clementine Trussel's first proper case as Mr Gout's apprentice. So far, things are not going well.

Called to a distant country house by mysterious letter, they arrive late and exhausted. But if they thought the resident's reception was cold, it only gets worse from there. Moments after they arrive they are attacked by the very creature they've been summoned to destroy.

It quickly becomes clear that not everything on the Thicklewood estate is what it seems. Mr Gout is suspicious of the story they've been told, and, somewhere, he's sure there is a body. But if Clementine and her master stand a chance of doing anything about it, first they must figure out exactly whom they can trust.

If they can't...then Clementine's first case might just end up being her last.

ACKNOWLEDGEMENT

Thanks to my wife Hayley, whose unending support and encouragement keep me going when I'm at my lowest.

Thanks again to Nick, my editor, who was quick to the task when I eventually delkivered this manuscript, over year late!

A special thanks to the booktok community, especially those who turn up again and again for my lives. Your support means this is all worth while!

ABOUT THE AUTHOR

M.a.knights

 Hello. I'm M.A.Knights, an English writer living in the glorious countryside of wild west Wales. Here the rugged cliffs, rolling hills and ever-changing sea inspire the worlds of my creation. After achieving a BSc in Countryside Conservation and an MSc in Geographic Information and Climate Change, I realised I am, in fact, not a scientist at all. It's the what-do-you-call-it? ... memory! Not what it used to be, don't you know? And what with all those numbers and things ... dreadful! Simply dreadful. So I've left the data crunching to those cleverer than I and instead have returned to the fantastical imaginings of my youth. I hope one day to lose myself in a world of my own creation.

I have developed a love for the farcical and absurd. Inspired by writers like Terry Pratchett, P.G.Wodehouse, Tom Holt and Jasper Fforde I revel in the creation of fantastical worlds full of improbable beasts and eccentric, larger than life characters.

Head to www.maknightswrites.co.uk for more information.

Printed in Great Britain
by Amazon

49471726R00108